THE S

OF FI R

(Android Wars – Book 1)

JJ TONER

Cover design: Anya Kelleye
Formatting: Karen Perkins

First Published November 15, 2020

Hardback edition ISBN 9781908519757
Paperback edition ISBN 9781908519764

THE SHAPE OF FEAR

PART 1 – PAIN

Chapter 1

Carla Scott was in the laboratory, peering into the eyes of Alpha Oscar 113, an Autonomic Unit.

When she was satisfied that the two cameras were perfectly aligned, she said, "Right, Oscar, focus on the building again."

The AU's cameras were focused on the seventh floor of a high rise 2,000 yards away, its lower stories swathed in smog. The images from the two cameras were projected side by side on her computer screen.

"Pick any window and look inside."

Oscar's cameras picked a window.

"Now, zoom in with both cameras." The images magnified. There were two figures inside, one male, one female. They appeared to be having an argument.

Carla laughed. "It's a pity we can't hear what they're saying."

Oscar began to lipread.

"What are you saying?"

"I can't keep covering for you."

"Since when?"

"Since day one."

The two figures circled one another, and Oscar lost sight of their faces.

Carla laughed again. "That's enough, Oscar, thank you. Let's try something different. I want you to maintain that view with your left eye but point the right one at the next window to the right."

The two images appeared on her screen. She directed Oscar to focus his right eye on windows further and further to the right until he couldn't go any further. The experiment was a success. The new cameras performed better than predicted, and Oscar's autofocus was outstanding, but his eyes looked very odd pointing in different directions.

Her X-Vid rang.

Lia's face appeared on the screen. "I am having difficulties preparing your meal," she said.

"What's the problem, Lia?"

"I am having difficulties preparing your meal."

"All right, Lia. I'll pick up something to eat on the way home." Carla checked her watch. "See you in thirty minutes."

She headed home, leaving Oscar in the capable hands of her assistant, Cassidy.

#

The apartment was a mess. Pieces of protein block and pools of water littered the kitchen floor. Lia was standing by the stove, clutching a knife in her left hand, a trail of hydraulic fluid all down the right side of her tunic and pants.

Her right hand was missing.

Carla placed her takeaway meal on the table and pried the knife from the AU's hand. Lia immediately moved to the table, tried to pick up the takeaway and swept it onto the floor. Then she dropped to her knees and tried to retrieve it.

"Leave it, Lia," said Carla. "You're injured. You can't function with one hand. Sit somewhere."

Lia sat on a kitchen chair.

Carla followed the trail of hydraulic fluid to the bedroom where she found the missing hand under her wardrobe. The heavy piece of furniture had toppled forward and fallen across the bed. She righted the wardrobe before turning her attention to the kitchen, picking up all the food and mopping the water and hydraulic fluid from the floor.

She removed the Unit's shirt. The hand was severed cleanly at the wrist, leaving a mass of dangling cables. Reattaching it should be a simple matter, but she would need her tools from the lab. She put Lia on recharge and thought about what had happened.

The AU must have been standing under the heavy wardrobe when it fell. She probably tried to stop it from falling and it severed her hand. She continued doggedly trying to prepare a meal, without realizing that her injury made it impossible.

Carla removed Lia's soiled clothes and dressed her in a shirt and pants from the wardrobe. She left her asleep the following day.

#

Cassidy suggested that Lia might have retained the sensation of the hand in the same way that amputees can "feel" their missing limb.

"Hmm, maybe," said Carla, "but I'm not sure our AUs have sensations."

"Or feelings."

"Or feelings. And how could she deny the evidence of her own eyes?"

Cassidy rubbed his beard with the pad of his thumb. "That's a tricky one. Have you spoken to Dr. Franck or the professor about it?"

"Not yet. I'm meeting Professor Jones tomorrow."

#

Her ex-boyfriend Stepan called and invited her to lunch. They met at her favorite fast food bar. He was already seated at a table when she arrived.

He stood up and gave her a brotherly hug. "How are you?"

"I'm fine. How have you been?" she said.

"I'm well. Very busy. We're loading a massive Constellation freighter."

"Still living alone?"

"Yes, how about you? Have you found anyone to replace me yet?"

"Still looking," she said, with a sweet smile.

Bartelli's was busy, as usual. Carla ordered a faux lasagna and iced fruitoid. Stepan chose the Pexcorn special protein cutlet.

As they ate, Stepan said, "Have you spoken with your father, recently?"

"Not recently."

"Have you tried to contact him?"

"Why should I?"

"He is your father."

"He spends a lot of time off-world. He's not too easy to contact."

Stepan frowned at her. "How long has it been since you spoke to him?"

"I haven't heard anything from him for nearly a year."

He pointed his fork at her. "You should send him a message. Someone needs to make the first move."

She stuffed her mouth to avoid any more discussion.

When she told Stepan what had happened to Lia the previous evening, he said, "Is she left-handed?"

"What do you mean?"

"You said the knife was in her left hand. Is she left-handed?"

"She's ambidextrous."

"Okay, so she carried on working in the kitchen with one hand missing? Why didn't she stop sooner? She must have realized that she couldn't manage with just one hand. And wasn't she in pain?"

Carla shrugged. "Her programming told her to cook my meal, and she wasn't aware her injury would make it impossible."

"That sounds like a serious design flaw." He made a sour face. "I hope you were nice to her. She is your friend, and she must have been upset."

"Why would she have been upset? Lia's an AU. She's an android – a machine."

"But she lost a hand! A whole hand. She must have lost a lot of blood."

"Not blood, Stepan. Hydraulic fluid."

"Even so, she must have been suffering. If it had happened to you or me, we would have screamed from the pain."

She shook her head. "Androids don't feel pain."

"I expect she cried her eyes out."

"Androids never cry," said Carla.

#

In her apartment that evening, Carla thought about her father. He had loved her once, back in the early days on Califon, before she turned ten. And before her mother left them. After the divorce, they abandoned their home on Califon, moving to the real California on Earth. Things had never been the same between them after that.

She put a hand into her pocket and took out her father's lighter. She treasured the ancient object. It was the only thing of his she had. She rubbed its smooth surface. She flipped it open, spun the wheel and was instantly rewarded with a smooth flame and a familiar smell that transported her back to her childhood. She flipped it shut, cutting off the flame, and put it back in her pocket. Then she keyed his number on her X-Vid, finger hovering over the call button. She tried to summon an opening greeting, but when she couldn't settle on one, she sent a text message instead.

HEY DAD, IT'S ME. ISN'T IT TIME WE MET? CALL ME. YOUR LOVING DAUGHTER, CARLA

Chapter 2

Carla thought about the problem. Lia was an excellent AU, a Mark 5 model. She could cook and clean, her heuristic program allowed her to learn new skills, and she had balance and poise. She even had some recognizable feminine qualities. But she was about as far removed from a human as an airplane was from a bird. After eight years working on the development of her androids, the gulf between them and humans was as wide as ever. Not that Xenodyne Automation had ever asked her to develop a complete replacement for a human being. On the contrary, every development had a strictly utilitarian – usually military – objective, under the overbearing weight of Federation funding.

They needed to feel pain.

The questions she had to answer were: In what way would an AU perform better if it could feel pain? Would pain give a military Unit an advantage in battle? And could she sell the idea to the military?

Pain could allow an Autonomic Unit to protect itself in battle. A fast reflex reaction to severe pain could save an AU from catastrophic damage in dangerous situations. She could foresee the need for an override switch to allow an AU to go through the pain barrier in extreme situations where necessary. The only remaining question was: could she find a way to do it?

After a half hour of winding down with Charlie Parker's saxophone, she went to bed and slept on the problem. She woke up convinced that it wouldn't take much to convey danger signals to the core data processor, using the android's Peripheral Nervous System.

After reattaching Lia's hand, reconnecting her broken lattice threads with a soldering iron, and patching up her skin, Carla replenished Lia's hydraulic fluid and woke her. She anticipated some questions from the AU about the loss and reattachment of her hand. There were none. Lia set about making Carla's breakfast as if nothing had happened. Carla found that disturbing, although she wasn't sure why.

#

Back in the lab, Alpha Oscar lay on the bench. She removed his Tesla powerpack. She was thinking about what Stepan had said. Lia was a machine, but did that make her any less entitled to compassion, to sympathy? And was she a friend?

She slid the AU's left eye camera from its socket and disconnected it.

I can disassemble Lia and put her back together again, she thought. *Does that make her any less real as a companion? Does an intimate knowledge of every one of her constituent parts make her any less lovable? Medical doctors have a similar detailed understanding of the component parts and organs of the human body, but that doesn't prevent them from forming lasting friendships. Or does it?*

Of course, a human can reciprocate friendship. An android can't. Although there are times when I wonder about that. She may be a machine I can switch on and off, but I'd miss her if I lost her. And even though she may be incapable of returning my feelings, I still love her. Lia is a friend!

She may be the only true friend I have.

#

That afternoon she took a hovercab to West Athens to meet with Josiah Jones, Professor of the School of Automation at Feynman Tech.

Carla had boundless respect for Professor Jones, an aged man with the enquiring mind of a sophomore, an unruly gray beard, and a rapidly diminishing head of hair. Jones's main claim to fame was a number of scientific articles co-authored as a student with an elderly Nobel Laureate.

"I haven't seen you for a while. What are you working on at the moment?"

"Improvements to the eyes – long-range focus and depth perception."

"And your assistant, Hopalong?"

"That's Cassidy. He's working with the Structural Section on the joints, the knees."

While the professor made coffee, she took a seat at his table and related the incident of the severed hand.

"She carried on with her work, you say, even though she was severely impaired?"

"Yes, Professor. The kitchen was like a bomb site."

The professor put two cups of coffee on the table and took a seat. "We have discussed this sort of thing before, have we not? In line with Xenodyne Automation corporate policy, the military AUs have limited functionality and built-in redundancy. Maintenance of the Units has never been a priority for the Federation."

"But what if this Unit had been armed with a lethal weapon? The risks are enormous."

"I have had a long-running argument with the corporation about this. There are so many obvious limitations to the AUs." He snorted. "If you ask me, all the military Units have is the ability to identify a target, point a weapon at it and pull the trigger." The professor's hand shook. Careful not to spill his coffee, he placed his cup on the table.

She laughed at his barbed sarcasm. "I believe the missing element is pain. The Units need to feel a sensation of pain—"

Professor Jones thumped the table with a palm, making Carla jump. "Bravo, young lady. You're right! There's been a shameless military bias in every XA development strand for years. There's so much missing from these programs. If I was running XA, physical sensations would be top of the agenda. Wait here." He hurried from the room and returned with a bundle of papers, placing them in front of her on the table. "I've been writing papers about that subject for years, but nobody would read them."

She leafed through the papers, reading the headings.

HUMAN CEREBRAL PROCESSING OF PAIN

REACTION DYNAMICS IN THE AUTONOMIC UNIT

TACTILE SENSATIONS FOR ARTIFICIAL INTELLIGENCE

THE ARTIFICIAL NERVOUS SYSTEM

PAIN AS THE GATEWAY TO FULL ARTIFICIAL INTELLIGENCE

Not all the articles carried Professor Jones's name. Some were really old. She remembered some of them from her college days; others she'd never seen before.

Struck, suddenly, by the size of the task she had set herself, she got up from the table. "Thank you, Professor. I'll take up no more of your time."

He waved her back into her chair. "I suggest that you concentrate on high threshold pain. What you need are receptors that respond only to intense mechanical stimulation such as cutting. Given how many inputs from the Peripheral Nervous System the core has to process already, you'll need to be careful not to overload it with too much data. Take a look at the first paper. It covers the processing of nociceptor inputs in the human cerebellum."

She glanced at the article. It was dated 2021, 305 years ago!

She stood up again, and he did the same. "I think we should keep it simple, don't you, Professor? I need to reprogram the pressure receptors to start with. When I have a workable solution, I'll think about how the Units might respond."

He picked up the papers and thrust them into her hands. "You'll need these."

Dismayed by the weight of the papers, she asked, "Have any of these been published?"

"Some of them were published, but not mine. No one would publish mine."

"Why not?"

He shrugged. "I guess they were ahead of their time. Either that or they didn't believe an old academic like me could have an original thought."

"Thank you for your time, Professor. And the coffee."

"You're welcome, Carla." He glanced at her cup. She hadn't touched it. "Let me know if there's anything more I can do to help. You've spoken with Fritz Franck about this?"

"Not yet. I doubt that he'll back it. He tends to be quite..."

"Focused on Xenodyne priorities?"

"I was going to say, 'narrow-minded.'"

The professor laughed and scratched his beard. "What you need is support from a board member. I'll sound out one of the directors on your behalf if you like."

"That would be wonderful. Thank you, Professor."

#

Returning to the lab, she outlined the meeting to Cassidy. She showed him the stack of academic papers.

"What are you proposing?" he said, after he'd run his eyes over them.

"We need something like a human nociceptive response. Most of the receptors in our bodies are triggered by physical injury; relatively few respond to pressure."

He said, "Like the pressure-sensitive lattice in the skin of the AUs."

"There are similarities, but the AU receptors feed into other functions, like orientation and balance. An adult female has about six million receptors, four and a half million of those in her skin, the rest associated with the internal organs."

Cassidy gave a low whistle.

"Our AUs wouldn't need anything like that

number. I'd say one every square centimeter should be sufficient."

Cassidy did a quick mental calculation. "That's still over twenty thousand. What about adult males?"

Carla laughed. "The same. Of course, the receptors are only the first part of the problem. We'll need to find a way to handle the new data stream. That'll be your job."

"No problem," said Cassidy with a grim smile. "I'll sort that out before lunch tomorrow."

Chapter 3

Dr. Fritz Franck was just about to light his second cigar of the day when his secretary stepped into his office.

"What is it, Lydda?"

"Carla Scott would like a word."

"Find her a slot next week sometime."

"She's waiting in my office."

He did his best to hide his annoyance, but he hated disruption to his daily routine. He had been head of the department for less than a year. She, on the other hand, had been with the department for over five years. In the interests of good staff relations, he would grant her an audience.

He placed the unlit cigar in his ashtray. "Very well, show her in."

When she came in, she took a seat without being invited.

"What can I do for you, Carla?"

"My personal Unit had an accident."

"An accident? In the lab?"

"At home."

"You have a Unit at home? Is this your own property?"

"Lia is company property. Why, is that a problem?"

"Never mind. What happened?"

"She lost a hand. A heavy piece of furniture fell on her. She carried on trying to make a meal. She made a terrible mess in the kitchen."

"You wish to apply for a replacement?" This was a waste of his time. "Speak to Lydda."

"No, no, Dr. Franck, I can repair her. I wanted to discuss a new development strand."

"I'm listening."

"Imagine a cowboy on horseback, driving a herd of steers along a cattle trail. Then imagine if he makes camp for the night and gets bitten by a rattlesnake. What would happen if he couldn't feel the bite?"

"I think we can safely assume that he would feel the bite of a rattlesnake."

"Yes, but just suppose that he couldn't."

"Why not?"

"That's not important. Use your imagination. He didn't feel the bite, okay?"

"If none of the other cowboys saw what had happened, he would die."

"Yes, he would die. So you see how important it is to be aware of an injury when it happens?"

He looked at his watch. "Will this take much longer?"

"Bear with me, please. What happens when one of our military AUs is injured in battle?"

"I don't know. It is replaced, I suppose."

"He carries on fighting, even though he may be severely impaired." She was waving her arms about as she spoke, now. "Unable to function properly, there is every likelihood that his actions will become uncontrolled and he will become a mortal danger to everyone, including those fighting on his own side. Until finally, he is abandoned on the battlefield."

He noticed how she used 'he' rather than 'it' to refer to the android. "Please get to the point."

"The point is my AU was unaware that she had sustained an injury."

'She' again.

"She carried on with her domestic duties as if nothing had happened. This is a major flaw in our Units, a flaw that could have lethal consequences for military AUs in battle."

Dr. Franck was speechless.

"I would like to research the possibility of making the AUs aware of their bodily make up, their physical limitations. They should know when they have been injured and know that they need to seek help."

"What are you suggesting? Pain receptors?"

Carla was the best android engineer on the planet, or so he'd been told, but if this was an example of her thinking, he doubted it. This whole conversation was totally off-beam.

"Yes, or something similar."

Suddenly he was aware that there was a cigar in his fist, its spine snapped in two. He couldn't even remember picking it up. He brushed the debris from his palm into the ashtray.

"Do I have to remind you how important your current work is? And how time-sensitive it is? I'm getting daily dispatches from the Federation generals looking for updates on your progress." She opened her mouth and said something unintelligible. He ignored her. "Nothing must be allowed to interfere with your work. Nothing. D'you hear me?"

As soon as she'd gone, he pressed the intercom on his desk. "Tell Major Grant I'd like to see him in my office." Picking a fresh cigar from the box, he lit it.

#

When Major Grant arrived, he lowered his heavy frame into the same seat that Carla had taken, again without being invited.

Dr. Franck had little regard for the security chief. They were of a similar age, but while Franck was thin as a pencil, Grant was clearly fighting a battle with his weight as his muscle turned to fat. It was a battle he was losing.

"Do you have anything for me, Major?"

"Meaning?"

"Any concerns about the security of the labs?"

Under his prominent brow, Grant's eyes narrowed, all but disappearing behind the flesh of his cheeks. "Why? Have you heard something I should know about?"

"No, I had nothing definite in mind. It was a general query. Your men patrol the building at night?" He opened his cigar box and offered it to Grant.

Grant waved the offer away. "Yes, of course. All entryways and exits are covered by surveillance cameras, and my men check the labs on foot every few hours. Why do you ask?"

"No reason. I had Carla Scott in here this morning. She informed me that she had an accident with an AU in her home. Did you know she has a Unit at home?"

"No, why should I?"

"The Unit is company property."

"And is that a problem? She is our number one android engineer."

"Do you know if anyone sanctioned the removal of an AU from the building?"

Grant's head sank below the level of his shoulders. He seemed to have no neck. "I assume your predecessor sanctioned it, if anyone did."

"Check it out for me, please."

Grant levered himself from the chair. "If there's nothing else..."

"There is just one more thing," said Dr. Franck. "I'd like you to keep an eye on Carla Scott."

Major Grant lifted an eyebrow. "Scott is a trusted employee of long standing..."

And I'm just a blow-in, thought Franck.

"Yes, yes. It's a simple precaution, based on a gut feeling. As a security man, you must know that sometimes you have to follow your gut, right?"

"Is there something you're not telling me, Fritz?"

"No, no. Some of her ideas are somewhat...ah...unorthodox. I just need to be sure she's singing the corporation anthem."

"You do know she was born off-world?" said the security chief.

"On Califon, yes, that's in her file. She was ten years old when she arrived on Earth."

Grant nodded. "I seem to recall her father was appointed to a senior Federation post."

#

Carla left Franck's office with her head reeling. She knew her work on visual acuity and depth perception could make a difference to all future AUs, but that it was of particular and pressing significance to the North Federation generals was a surprise. An unpleasant surprise.

Cassidy asked her how the meeting went, and she told him, "Franck's reaction was entirely predictable. The guy can't see beyond the end of his cigar."

Cassidy snorted. "He's out of his depth. They should never have given him the job. He's nothing but a pen-pusher, a miserable bean counter. They should have given the job to a qualified engineer."

"Yes, well, they did, and we have to live with him."

"I thought they might have given it to you."

She laughed. "Why me? I'm not management material."

"No one is better qualified."

"You're too kind, but I would never have taken the job. You know me. I'm only happy when I'm tinkering with my androids."

"And nobody's better at it than you, Carla. You're the original and best android whisperer in the Federation. They couldn't lose your expertise."

She dismissed his flattery with a wave. Then she told him what Dr. Franck had said about the importance of their work to the North Federation military. "He was so worked up, he shredded one of his cigars."

Cassidy laughed. "So our Pain project is dead in the water?"

"Not at all. Professor Jones has promised to talk to a board member about it. Franck may find himself out-voted."

"And what if the military are not convinced?"

"That may be an issue, but I'd be confident of talking them around to the idea. Who needs a soldier that doesn't know when he's wounded?"

"I'm convinced," said Cassidy, but the expression on his face told her otherwise.

She said, "We have to face the possibility of a war between two armies of androids. Imagine what that would be like if no one on the battlefield could feel any pain."

"Sounds like a recipe for chaos. Thousands of AUs would be wiped out."

"Not just AUs, Cassidy. Human lives would be lost, too. Anyone within reach of their weapons would be annihilated."

"I'm convinced," he said, and this time she knew that he meant it.

Chapter 4

The freighter *Vladivostok* moved out of Earth's orbit and approached the Interstellar Gate (AD). On the bridge, Captain Korskov keyed in his security access codes and gave the order to his executive officer. The conventional engines wound down and stopped. Warning klaxons sounded across the entire ship. Forty seconds later, the massive ship drifted through the Gate. The captain and his crew had braced themselves as soon as the klaxons sounded, but still every heart on board skipped a beat as they entered the fifth dimension; no one ever got used to that jolt.

The moment the XO engaged the Brazill Drive, an unnatural silence enveloped the ship, and the crew settled down for the 10-day journey through the Conduit to their home base, 263 light years away in the D-System.

The ship carried twelve flesh and blood crewmen and ten Souther androids, or Popovs. In her vast cargo bays, she carried a wide variety of goods: two million tons of Pexcorn Foods protein blocks, building materials, rare metals, priceless art, and mail. Most important of all, she carried one VIP: the Food Commissioner for the Norther Federation Alliance, his secret mission: to meet his counterpart in the Souther Bloc to help lubricate the wheels of the trade negotiations.

As the long, tedious journey through the Interstellar Conduit progressed, the onboard temperature fell. The captain and crew donned their winter clothing. The ordinary crewmen slept between patrols of the cargo bays; the bridge crew blew on their hands and played card games.

Nothing much happened for 20 hours. In his cabin, the captain spent his time composing a difficult letter to the mistress he'd left behind on Earth. His wife, Svetlana, was waiting for him on Marxina. She hadn't seen him for 15 standard months, and his mistress would probably never see him again. His words dissolved on the X-Vid in front of him. He rubbed his eyes and popped his ears in an attempt to mitigate the effects of 'interdimensional fug.' After years of journeys like this one, he was familiar with that uncomfortable feeling, the sensation that his body was wrapped in cotton wool, all senses deadened and normal time in suspension. The *Vladivostok* was like a ghost ship drifting in silence through a mild haze, manned by a ghostly crew, speaking in flat, muted voices that no bulkheads could echo.

His XO knocked on the cabin door and stepped in. "All well, Captain?"

The captain nodded. "Anything to report?"

"Nothing to worry about. The temperature has

dropped close to freezing. I've had a few minor complaints from some of the younger crewmen."

"Remind them how much their bonuses are."

The XO grinned. "I did that, Captain. I came to tell you that the cook has a meal ready. Do you want it served in here?"

"I'll come down to the mess." He closed his X-Vid and the two men made their way to the mess hall.

The ghostly murmur of the voices of eight crewmen – about half the ship's complement – filled the mess hall. The captain and his XO took their places at the captain's table and the cook sprang to attend to them.

"Welcome, Captain. On the menu today, I have diced lamb stew or lemon sole."

The captain never ceased to be amazed at the variety of dishes his cook could concoct from a basic protein block and vegetable paste. He decided to opt for the lamb stew, but before he could convey his choice to the cook, the ship juddered.

"What was that?" said the XO.

Then the two officers were sprinting back to the bridge. The juddering had felt like a landing, but the ship hadn't landed anywhere in ten years, and there was nowhere to land in an Interstellar Conduit.

The bridge crew was busy checking all systems.

"Report," said the captain.

"All systems appear normal, Captain," replied the senior bridge officer.

"Something hit us," the captain barked. "Check for hull breaches, all decks."

"Aye aye, Captain."

A few moments later, the senior bridge officer reported, "Everything looks nominal out there, Captain, apart from two exterior cameras on the left lateral cargo array that are no longer functioning."

"Get a repair crew out there," said the XO.

"Captain!" cried one of the crew monitoring the cargo bays. "The doors on Cargo Bay F17 are showing open."

The XO bounded across to the monitoring screens. "He's right, Captain. Whatever we hit has damaged the doors."

"What's in that cargo bay?" said the captain.

The cargo man responded, "Protein blocks, Captain. Fifty-thousand tons of it."

"Get a repair crew down there, XO."

"Aye aye, Captain," said the XO. "Should we stop the Brazill Drive?"

"No need," said the captain. "We may have lost some of the protein, but if we have, I'm not going back for it."

The XO selected two crew members to repair the doors on Cargo Bay F17, Leading Crewman Agipov and Ensign X35. The crewman was kitted up in a full suit. The ensign was an android; he went as he was. The XO briefed them before they made their way down to the cargo compartments in the bowels of the ship. Their orders were to check out the doors and see if they could repair the cameras.

Checking the pressure monitor panel on the inner airlock door, the two crewmen confirmed that the outer bay doors of Cargo Bay F17 had been compromised. The bay was open and venting cargo into the fifth dimension.

"We're going in," said the leading crewman. He opened the inner door. Man and android stepped into the inner airlock, vented it and stepped through into the cargo bay.

On the bridge, the captain and his XO waited anxiously for word from the repair crew.

The XO pressed the ship-wide intercom. "Report, Agipov."

The captain reminded him that external radio communications were non-operational in the fifth dimension. The XO swore. "I thought we'd still be able to reach Agipov's suit radio."

The captain shook his head. "We just have to be patient. Keep an eye on the cargo bay's internal airlock indicator. That will tell you when they're back inside. And don't worry, I'm sure they'll do the job. They're both good men."

Ten minutes went by. Then the inner airlock was activated.

"They're coming back in," said the XO.

The captain checked the cargo door monitor. "They haven't closed the outer doors. They're still breached."

"Captain!" said one of the bridge crew.

"What is it, crewman?" said the XO.

"Sir, I turned one of the rearview cameras. I now have a partial external view of the cargo bay. You need to see this."

The XO gasped at what he saw. A smaller ship had attached itself onto the side of the freighter, its fins clearly visible. "Close the inner airlock."

"Too late for that, XO," said the captain. "We've been boarded."

The XO gave the order to issue arms.

The captain countermanded the order. "Blasters won't work in this dimension, remember?"

The XO looked crestfallen. "Is there nothing we can do?"

"Fetch the Food Commissioner from his cabin, quickly," said the captain.

Chapter 5

Carla set off for the lab on foot first thing the following morning. The sun had barely risen; the birds were putting the finishing touches to their dawn chorus. On her way past Feynman Tech she passed a group of students preparing for a protest demonstration. Some of their protest signs read:

DEMOCRACY IS NOT FOR SALE
COLONIES ARE FOR EVERYONE
BAN MONOPOLIES
PROTEIN BLOCKS ARE NOT FOOD
JOIN ANTIX

It seemed the resistance to the Federation in general and Xenodyne Industries in particular were as vigorous as ever.

When she arrived at the lab, she made a pot of coffee and tuned in to her most creative thoughts. On the face of it, the solution seemed obvious. The lattice of conductive threads that made up the Peripheral Nervous System (PNS) of the AU was sensitive to pressure. All she had to do was adapt the technology to identify any break in the lattice.

All she had to do! She laughed. It sounded so simple.

She wrote up the concept in vague terms on the assumption that a suitable solution would emerge from developments in the lab. Costings and timescales were based on a set of wild estimates and projections that were nothing short of pure guesswork.

As she worked, she pondered the nature of the Autonomic Units. She'd worked on AU developments for eight years – five in the lab and three before that at Feynman Tech – and she'd always thought of the AU as a machine. Why had she never considered attempting anything like this before? Pain was a human quality. If the development was a success, perhaps it might be the first of many. The addition of other human traits – emotions, perhaps – could open up a world of possibilities for AUs. She was reminded of the story of Pinocchio, a wooden doll who wanted to become human, like other children. What would an AU with emotions be like? Could it be equal to a human, with feelings? Could she build an AU that experienced joy, sadness, fear, anger, trust, suspicion, curiosity? What about empathy, hatred and love, intelligence, and – the holy grail of machine intelligence – consciousness?

Cassidy was late.

"What kept you?" she said.

"I had to drop Sophie off at a student

demonstration," he replied. "She's an active member of ANTIX."

"Are you a member?"

"No, but Sophie tells me the movement is growing every day."

Carla was surprised. The phrase 'biting the hand that feeds you' sprang to mind. She said nothing. Instead, she transferred a copy of her draft proposal onto his X-Vid. While he read it, she made him a cup of coffee and topped up her own.

"It's a good proposal," said Cassidy, "but I don't think XA will fund it."

"Why not, if it's a good idea?"

"Your costings for one thing. How solid are they? What are 'miscellaneous sundries'?" He circled the offending item with his electronic pen.

She flapped her hands at him. "Of course, the costings are rough. What did you expect? It's a first draft, an outline proposal."

"It's very rough."

"Yes, all right, forget the costings. What do you think about the idea?"

Cassidy ran his fingers through his hair. "The basic idea is fine, but programming the reactions to pain will be challenging, to put it mildly. I reckon you could double these cost estimates."

"I thought we could start with the enemy fire response and adapt that."

"It's hardly the same thing, is it, Carla? Returning enemy fire is all tied into the Perception module. This is so much more complex. Even at the high threshold the receptors will need to be sensitive enough to detect injury, and any serious injury will break the threads of the lattice. How will it be possible to transmit any information to the central core along broken threads?"

She hadn't thought of that. Cassidy's objection was sound.

"You're out of your mind. You do realize that, don't you?" he said.

She snatched the proposal back. "I'll double the costs."

#

She sent the proposal to Professor Jones.

His reaction was positive but guarded. "It's rather vague, Carla. To get funding it will need something more concrete. You should include some specific ideas."

"I kept it vague on purpose," she said. "I don't have a lot of specifics at this stage."

"You could mention the Peripheral Nervous System."

"I'd prefer not to. We may need something entirely different."

"Like what?"

"I don't know."

The professor blinked. "Okay, why not mention the Orientation module?"

"Same answer."

"What other module could handle it?"

"I don't know yet, but you said yourself there is a danger of overload."

"And what? You might have to build a new dedicated module?"

"The thought had occurred to me, yes."

The professor paused. "All right, Carla, but please put something concrete in there, something that I can talk about to the people who hold the purse strings."

The call ended, and Carla set about adjusting her proposal. By the end of the day she had completed a revised proposal featuring PREM, a 'Pain Response Electronic Module.' It was still nothing but a 'black box' with no real substance, described in general terms vague enough to allow for any of three possible solutions: reprogramming of the Orientation module, a hardware extension of the existing modules, or the development of an entirely new hardware module.

She sent the revised proposal to Professor Jones.

#

Cassidy arrived home to find Sophie sitting on the bed in tears.

He put his arm around her shoulders. "What's the matter, Sophie?"

She rubbed a sleeve across her eyes. "The demonstration... The police..."

"What? The police broke up your demonstration? Are you injured?"

She shook her head. "They fired teargas and attacked us with batons. I was lucky, I got away."

"I thought it was supposed to be a peaceful protest," he said.

"It was, until the cops arrived. A lot of them weren't even real cops. They were..."

"Autonomic Units?"

"Androids, yes. We tried to reason with them, but how can you reason with an android?"

Chapter 6

Captain Korskov of the freighter *Vladivostok* had been locked up in his cabin for two days without food. His cabin was equipped with hot and cold running water, so he wasn't dying of thirst, but the pains in his stomach and concern for his crew and his VIP passenger kept him awake during the sleep cycle. The last thing he'd done before surrendering his vessel to the pirates was to disguise the Food Commissioner as a member of the crew. It was all he could do, but he doubted that the rest of the crew could be relied upon to keep his secret.

The cabin door opened, and a surly stranger appeared, armed with an antique handgun. "Come with me, Captain."

Blasters were useless in the fifth dimension, but the pirates carried ancient percussion weapons, and they worked fine. There was a dead crewman in the Food Commissioner's cabin to prove it.

The stranger escorted Korskov to the bridge and deposited him in front of another stranger – a thin long-haired individual, wearing a red morning coat with elaborate brass buttons and matching red bandana – lounging in the captain's chair, eating a fruit bar.

This is the man who stole my ship, he thought, bile rising from his empty stomach.

"Help yourself," said bandana-man, pointing to a pile of fruit bars on the chart table.

The captain picked up two bars and began to devour them. He was starving.

"I want to thank you for the cargo, Captain," said the pirate chief. "It will keep my crew fed for a standard year."

The captain managed a few words between mouthfuls. "This is piracy. There are rules protecting ships in space."

"I think the phrase you're searching for is free enterprise. It's what I do."

"Who are you?" said the captain.

"They call me Captain Blackmore."

Captain Korskov knew the name. He had heard all the stories. Blackmore was the most notorious space pirate in the Six Systems, plying his trade in normal space and on every Interstellar Conduit. Every Conduit, that is, except the AD one, which was protected at both ends by supposedly unbreakable access codes. There was a price on Blackmore's head. The captain couldn't remember how much it was, but he knew it was enough to retire on, comfortably.

He said, "My cargo was part of a brokered deal between the trade negotiators on Califon. Stealing it could start a Federation war."

"That's not my problem, Captain."

"Surely you don't expect to get away with it?"

BIackmore smiled. "I do. I will. I have."

The captain pointed a finger at the pirate. "You and your crew will be seized the minute you emerge from the Conduit on either end."

"Let me worry about that."

"You will be hunted down by the Federation military. There's no place to hide anywhere in the Six Systems."

"You're probably right, which is why you won't find me hiding anywhere in the Six Systems."

The captain was dumbfounded by this statement. If Blackmore had found somewhere to hide that wasn't in any of the Six Systems of the Federation, the captain couldn't imagine where that could be, and that would certainly explain why the pirates had never been caught.

"I'd like my crew looked after," said the captain. "They will need food and water."

"Of course. We may be pirates, but we're not monsters."

Captain Korskov doubted that, but he bit his lip. "Where did you get the access codes to the AD Conduit?"

"That's for me to know and you to find out," said Captain Blackmore. "Have another fruit bar. They're really good."

The captain took two more.

"What am I going to do with you?" said the pirate chief. "I'm inclined to let you and your crew go, but I need your ship to transport the cargo back to my base. You see the problem."

"Do you have another ship that we could use?"

Blackmore shook his long hair from his eyes. "Unfortunately, no. We have the *Missie Bess*, but we've had her for a long time and the crew is attached to her."

"We could return her to you after we've reached the D-System."

"How would you manage that?"

"You could send one of your men with us. He could take the ship back to your base after dropping us off."

Blackmore scratched his chin. "That might work...On the other hand, it might be easier all round to simply flush the lot of you out the nearest cargo door."

#

Dressed in ill-fitting clothing borrowed from a crewman, and doing his best to merge with the crew, the Food Commissioner was less than comfortable. He was locked up along with the XO and the crew, in Cargo Bay F17, a bay that had lost a significant portion of its cargo of protein blocks. They had no contact with the pirates apart from when they were given food and water through the internal airlock. This happened twice a day when the XO did his best to get some information from them. The XO's main concern was for the safety of the captain, but none of his questions were answered.

The pirates had no use for the ten crew members who were androids; they were powered down and their valuable powerpacks removed. The Food Commissioner found the crewmen's reaction to this surprising. They seemed to regard the disposal of the androids as an act of casual violence. He imagined the crew had had too many shared experiences with the androids over too long a period not to regard them as anything other than equals. And they obviously feared being disposed of in the same casual way themselves.

Of all the men in the cargo hold, the Food Commissioner knew he was the least likely to survive. His secret identity was an ace in the hole, something that might save the ass of the XO or any one of the crew.

After three days, the airlock opened, and a group of armed pirates entered the cargo bay. The leader was a lanky, long-haired individual wearing red. He introduced himself as Captain Blackmore.

"Where is our captain?" said the XO.

"Your captain is in his cabin," said Blackmore. "I have been discussing with him what we should do with you men."

The crew exchanged nervous glances.

"I'd like to speak with Captain Korskov," said the XO.

"All in good time," the pirate chief replied. "First, I have a proposition to put to you all. I'm offering every one of you the opportunity of a lifetime."

The crew remained silent.

"What could be better than a life among the stars, every day a celebration of life and freedom? I'm offering you a chance to join us."

The crew began to speak among themselves.

"You mean you don't intend to release us?" said the XO.

"I can't do that. I don't have a suitable vessel for you."

"You could take the cargo and let us continue on our original course," said the XO.

Captain Blackmore shook his head. "You will appreciate the difficulty I am in. I don't have a ship big enough to off-load all the cargo."

"These men have wives and families in the D-System. You can't ask them to abandon everything."

"That's the only offer on the table," said the pirate captain. "Each man must decide for himself."

"And what if they refuse?"

"In that case, I will have no choice. I will leave you to talk it out among yourselves." Captain Blackmore turned on his heels, and he and his men left the cargo bay.

Chapter 7

Two days after submitting her revised proposal to the professor, Carla rang him and asked him what he thought of it.

"It's much better. I like your PREM module. I take it this is a new hardware module?"

"Only if necessary," said Carla. "Have you spoken with any of the directors?"

"I spoke to Ricarda Petrik. She was very interested in the idea and asked to be kept in the loop."

Carla's heartbeat doubled. Petrik was CFO of Xenodyne Automation. Carla had met her several times and liked her. "Thank you, Professor. Should I send her my proposal?"

"Yes, send it to her. And be sure to send a copy to Dr. Franck."

Carla closed the X-Vid. Her scalp tingled with a mixture of apprehension and excitement. The project was more than a distant hope, now! Petrik was an influential woman. With her backing it would have every chance of being funded. But would she be able to pull it off?

"That was the professor?" said Cassidy.

"Yes. He's sold the idea to Ricarda Petrik."

Cassidy swore quietly. "You mean we may actually have to do this?"

#

She submitted her revised proposal to Dr. Franck with a copy to Ricarda Petrik, and immediately began to spend every spare moment working on the receptors.

Her first tentative ideas were too complicated, but after sleeping on the problem she came up with the glimmer of an idea. Perhaps she could use the longitudinal lines of the PNS lattice to identify and isolate severe damage, ignoring the lateral lines altogether. She discussed the idea with Cassidy while she tinkered with the camera alignment of her test subject, Alpha Oscar, sitting on her work surface.

"How are we going to do that?" was Cassidy's first question.

Thinking on her feet, Carla said, "The process could manage separate pulses from the core along each major route. Down an arm, for example, each longitudinal line would have its own set of signals." She traced a finger down the AU's arm.

"How many threads are we talking about?"

"We could limit it to two threads per centimeter. That's forty down each arm, and about two hundred for the torso and legs. Say... three hundred in total."

"Okay, but how would it work?"

She shook her head. "I haven't worked that out, yet."

Cassidy gave it some thought. Then he said, "Could we use miniaturized Electrical Time-Domain Reflectometers?"

Carla was stunned by this suggestion. The ETDR was a hand-held instrument used to isolate breakages in communications lines. It operated on the principle that when an electrical pulse encountered a breach in a line it was reflected back. The instrument used the time delay between transmission and receipt of the reflection to calculate the position of the breach.

Carla grabbed Cassidy by his ears and kissed him on the forehead. "You're a genius!"

He blushed. "But what if there are two breaks in one line? The first one would mask the second one."

She beamed at him. "That's a problem for another day. I want you to think about how our AU will react when he senses pain."

"You mean a broken vertical line in his lattice."

"Yes, pain."

Sitting on Carla's work surface, Alpha Oscar turned his head and stared, unblinking and slightly cross-eyed, at Carla for a long moment. Then his head turned back to its original position.

#

Carla had sworn Cassidy to silence, but he found it impossible not to say anything to his partner. Sophie was a registered nurse, and they often discussed the parallels between her flesh-and-blood patients and Cassidy's mechanical ones.

She was intrigued by the story of Lia's accident. "The android was unaware that she'd lost a hand?"

"Yes, she felt nothing."

"There's a rare medical condition where a person can feel no pain. It's called CIP, Congenital Insensitivity to Pain. I've seen two cases in my career so far."

"Sounds like a recipe for an early death."

"That's true. The life expectancy of these patients is severely limited. It might be helpful to examine this condition and see how it affects the patient."

"How is it treated?" he asked.

"It's a genetic condition. There are gene therapies available, although they involve extensive gene research and can only be accessed by those with bottomless wallets. Everyone else with the condition must look after themselves very carefully."

Cassidy went off to investigate the condition. He discovered that failure of the joints was a common problem for people with CIP. There were direct applications to his work on android knees, but that would require the addition of a Visceral Nervous System to protect the limbs and joints from physical trauma.

Chapter 8

Major Grant, the head of security at XA, barged into the lab. A bull of a man with the beginnings of a paunch and a military-style crew cut, he was one of the few employees with free access to every part of the building.

He looked around the lab. "Where's Carla Scott?"

"She's at a meeting with the cam team. She should be back in about an hour," said Cassidy.

"Come with me." Grant's tone left little room for refusal.

Cassidy had been half expecting something like this ever since Carla had gone over Franck's head in submitting her proposal to the CFO. He followed the major to Franck's office.

Major Grant closed the door. Then he led Cassidy across the room and sat him down in a chair facing Franck's desk.

"Carla Scott is at a meeting," said Grant to Franck.

Franck fixed his beady eyes on Cassidy. "I've had a memorandum from the board. They are looking for an urgent progress report on your work."

This was clearly a lie. Carla made regular monthly reports, the latest no more than two weeks prior. Franck was playing some game.

Cassidy replied, "I can only speak for myself. As Carla mentioned in her last report, things are going well. I have nearly completed the trials on a new locking mechanism for the knee joints."

Franck glowered at him. "What is the top running speed of the AU? Remind me again."

"A military grade Unit can exceed seventeen miles per hour."

"For how long?"

"On a full power charge, they can sustain that speed for fifty to fifty-five minutes. But any reduction in speed will allow them to keep going for much longer."

"The slower they move, the longer they can last?"

Cassidy was feeling more and more uneasy. Franck was fully aware of the operational parameters of the military Units. "Yes sir, on a logarithmic scale. I'm sure you have all the figures on file."

Franck gave Cassidy his creepy smile. "We've had an order from the Federation military command. They are pushing for more."

"More speed? I'm not sure that's possible. Seventeen miles per hour is better than twelve seconds for the hundred-yard sprint."

Franck continued as if Cassidy hadn't spoken. "They want longer sustained performance at top speed."

Cassidy snorted. "We'd need to develop a bigger powerpack, for a start."

"Precisely. When can you start?"

Cassidy shook his head. "With all due respect, sir, these Units are not indestructible. Even on an athletics track, I doubt their frames could survive any more treatment like that. Over rough terrain, up and down hills, they'd be shaken to pieces."

"Those are our orders," said Franck. "And they're looking for a higher sprint speed."

"They want better than twelve seconds for a hundred yards?"

"Yes."

"I'm not sure that's even possible."

Grant interjected at that point, "Marines can do three miles in twenty-seven minutes and I, myself, have done the hundred yards in better than eleven seconds."

Cassidy scoffed. He did a quick mental calculation. "Three miles in twenty-seven minutes is a mere seven miles an hour."

"The Autonomic Units are better than humans in every way, are they not?" said Franck.

"Physically better, yes, but there are limits."

Franck's smile broadened. "At the end of the day, the only limits are those imposed by our own imaginations. Don't you agree?"

Cassidy said nothing. The question was rhetorical.

Grant said, "You were seen recently at a student demonstration. I hope you're not a member of the

Resistance. The corporation would take a dim view if you were."

Cassidy squirmed under Grant's glare. "I was showing solidarity with my girlfriend."

Franck waved a hand in dismissal. The meeting was over. He turned to Grant. "You had something else to discuss, Major?"

#

When Carla returned to the lab, Cassidy told her about the meeting.

"That's Franck's way of interfering with our 'pain' proposal. I doubt if those new orders are real."

She put a call through to Franck's secretary, Lydda.

"Dr. Franck has issued new orders to my assistant. I'd like to see those new orders in writing."

"I'll pass your request to Dr. Franck," said Lydda and she terminated the call.

Cassidy said, "What do we do now?"

"We carry on in secret. Until I see these new orders on my X-Vid screen, we ignore them. I'll continue with my work on vision. You must carry on working on your knees."

Cassidy smiled at the witticism.

Chapter 9

Carla watched the news with increasing alarm. Inter-colony trade, the glue that kept the Federation together, was breaking down. Cries of foul from the Southers' delegation were matched by threats from the Northers to abandon the talks altogether and take the next flight home.

Carla's birth planet, Califon in the C-System, had been selected as the ideal location to host the talks, and she thought it was. Her memories of the planet had long since faded as she'd left the system at the age of ten standard (Earth) years, when her father relocated to Earth. But the planet was universally regarded as a paradise, with a comfortable climate, invigorating gravity, a short solar cycle, and a population of young colonists, evenly split between Northers and Southers.

After half a century of trade talks, the two sides were farther apart than ever, and ready to tear one another limb from limb. Under the terms of the nascent agreement, the Northers had agreed to ship a consignment of much-needed raw materials and supplies from Earth to Leninets in the D-System, using a Souther freighter. But when the enormous Constellation freighter, its crew and cargo failed to arrive at the D-System at the end of their 10-day transit, the fragile talks collapsed. Every concession previously agreed was withdrawn. Compromise positions that had taken more than a generation to negotiate were torn up. The two sides were at loggerheads.

A military search was initiated from Leninets. Using their fastest fighters, it would take eight days to traverse the AD Conduit from the D Gate to the A Gate. Every citizen of the Federation held their breath in hopes that the freighter could be found. Perhaps its Brazill Drive had failed and it would be discovered drifting somewhere in the Conduit.

Both the president of the Norther Federation Alliance and the premier of the Souther Federation Bloc appealed for calm and for the delegates to return to the negotiating table. In speeches remarkably similar in content and tone, they each spoke of compromise and goodwill, of patience and perseverance. Carla sensed that their conciliatory language disguised thinly veiled threats to go to war. The Spalding-Paviaski Accord had eliminated nuclear weapons over two centuries earlier, but each side had huge android armies and enough conventional arms and ordnance to destroy a planet, or a system. If war broke out, the Federation – administered jointly by both sides – would be the first casualty, placing billions on both sides of the divide at risk of death by swift annihilation or slow starvation.

Cassidy called Carla on her X-Vid. "Are you watching this?" he said.

"Yes. Can you hear the sound of sabers rattling?"

"Loud and clear. It's difficult to imagine what they are hoping to gain by their actions."

"Who, the Northers?" she said.

"Who else?"

"I don't know. It might not be them. It could be engine failure."

"Whatever it was, this makes our work more important than ever."

"And more urgent," said Carla.

After that call, she rang her father again and left a message on his X-Vid. "It's Carla, Dad. Call me. I still have your lighter. You never explained what it was for."

Chapter 10

Eight days later, the Southers' fleet had completed the search of the Conduit and found no trace of the missing freighter. Scientists were baffled. Given that the only way a spacecraft could leave any Interstellar Conduit was through a Gate, and each Conduit had just two Gates, one at each end, no one could explain what had happened. The ship's disappearance was all the more alarming since the AD Conduit was used exclusively by Southers' spacecraft, protected by unbreakable security codes known only to the captains of the Southers' freighters and military battle fleet. It seemed the unbreakable security codes had been broken. Either that or some of the established science around the fifth dimension and the Conduits was in need of revision.

In the lab, Cassidy had built a crude software version of an ETDR, and Carla was still working her way through the professor's academic papers.

Stepan called to invite Carla to lunch.

Carla snapped at him, "I'm busy. We've just taken on a massive new project."

"All the more reason to take a break," said

Stepan. "You need to eat to keep your strength up and feed your brain."

She agreed to meet him at Bartelli's.

Cassidy threw a skeptical look in Carla's direction.

"What?" she said.

"You're having lunch with Stepan again!"

"So what?"

"You getting back together with your ex?"

She scoffed. "He's a friend, nothing more."

#

Bartelli's was busy, as usual. Stepan ordered a protein steak and green vegetables. Carla chose her usual faux lasagna and glass of chilled fruitoid.

They spoke about the missing freighter. Stepan said, "It's hard to believe that a spacecraft as big as a Constellation freighter could just disappear. There was close to three million tons of cargo onboard."

Stepan was a docks manager. She asked if he had been involved with the loading of the cargo.

"Yes, I supervised a gang of your AUs loading some of the protein blocks onto the shuttlecraft."

The food arrived and they began to eat.

"Now, what can I do for you?" he said, between mouthfuls.

"You invited me, remember? Not the other way around."

"Yes, but you wouldn't have come if you didn't want to ask me something."

She nodded. "Very preceptive. I do have a problem that you might be able to help me with. We are working on enhancements to the AUs."

"What sort of enhancements?"

"Feelings."

His eyes opened wide in amazement. "Emotions?"

"Not emotions, feelings. Specifically, the feeling of pain. An AU feels no pain."

"You mean like Lia's accident with the wardrobe?"

"Yes. An AU can place his hand into a naked flame and leave it there until there's nothing left. He feels nothing."

Stepan took a minute to absorb that idea. "That's not good. You want to fix that?"

"That's the plan."

His brows furrowed. "How can an android feel pain?"

"You know the android skin is made from a special piezoelectric polymer that's pressure-sensitive? It's called the Peripheral Nervous System."

"Hold on, you lost me. What's a piezoelectric polymer?"

"It's a special material that creates a small electric pulse when compressed. A lattice of conducting threads crisscrossing the skin picks up these electric pulses and conveys them to the core."

"Okay, I've got that. How can you use that for pain?"

"We need to use the lattice to pick up any physical injury to the skin."

"So what's your problem?"

"I need to decide how to program a reaction to an injury once the signals reach the core."

"Like an emotional reaction? A reflex?"

"If you like, yes. How do you react to pain?"

"Whenever I'm injured, I yell. I jump away. If it's a serious injury, I yell my head off. I scream."

"Okay. Then what?"

"Then I attend to the injury, put my hand on it, bandage it, or call for help."

"Right." She waved a fork at him. "But what happens in between the yell and the bandage?"

"Nothing."

"Think carefully," said Carla. "There's pain. What is your first reaction?"

"I put my hand on the injury..."

"Before that, what do you feel?"

"I don't know. Worried? Annoyed? Angry?"

At the end of the meal, Carla ordered a pot of tea. Stepan ordered a beer. The waitress arrived with the drinks on a tray. She placed Stepan's beer on the table. Stepan wrapped his fingers around his glass, placing his other hand flat on the table. As the waitress placed Carla's teapot down, some of the scalding hot tea splashed from the spout onto Stepan's hand.

He screeched and jumped up, pulling his hand to his chest. His chair fell backward with a clatter. Leaping to her feet, Carla grabbed his glass and threw the beer over the back of his hand, soaking her sweatshirt.

"What did you do that for?" he yelled at her.

Everyone in the restaurant turned to see what the row was about. The waitress apologized. "I'm really sorry, sir."

"It's nothing," said Stepan, brushing the worst of the liquid from his chest.

The waitress picked up the chair and hurried away to fetch a replacement for Stepan's beer.

"I'm sorry, Stepan." Carla covered her mouth to hide her amusement. "I was only trying to help."

"You're mad, Carla. It wasn't that serious." He sat down again, clutching the back of his hand.

They finished their meal in silence.

Before they parted, she apologized again. "I don't know what came over me. I thought it was a good idea."

He gave her a hug. "Forget it, Carla. It was nothing."

#

Cassidy was excited. "A message came through from Ricarda Petrik's office. The PREM project has been approved."

Carla's reaction was one of relief. "Now we can give the project the time it deserves."

Cassidy wasn't so sure. "Is Franck on board with this? I think he will still insist that we meet all our existing deadlines."

"Let me worry about that," said Carla.

"How was your lunch date with your boyfriend?" he said.

"He's not my boyfriend," she replied. "Our meeting was very productive."

"Sounds good. So you'll be meeting him again for more lunches?"

"I don't think so. I emptied his beer all over his sweater."

"Why? Were you having an argument?"

By way of celebration, she plugged her earbuds in. "Not at all. We were talking. The waitress spilled hot, scalding tea on his hand. It was an accident. I threw his beer over his hand. He shouted at me. It was nothing. We parted as friends."

"And how was that productive?"

"I saw his initial reaction. In his eyes. That told me all I needed to know. By the time he'd jumped up, he was shocked, but shock wasn't his initial reaction."

"Okay, tell me," he said.

"His initial reaction was fear." She selected a Duke Ellington track on her X-Vid.

Cassidy looked dejected. "Fear. You want to simulate fear in our AUs?"

"Not simulate. I want our AUs to feel fear."

He shook his head. "Is that even possible?"

"That's the challenge that faces us," she said. "Without that initial reaction our pain receptors will be useless. And think where we could go when we succeed? Fear will be the AU's first real emotion."

"You mean *if* we succeed. You said 'when.'"

"I know what I said, and I know what I mean." Smiling, she turned up the volume on her earbuds. "Have faith, Cassidy."

PART 2 – FEAR

Chapter 11

After a couple of days of intense work, Carla and her assistant were ready for their first major trial. Alpha Oscar, their test subject, lay on Carla's workbench. He was in sleep mode, but with his powerpack fully charged. A multichannel digital storage oscilloscope connected wirelessly to his core allowed Carla to observe the steady flow of multiple pulses of high frequency alternating current, indicating a fully intact skin on all parts of the AU's exoskeleton frame.

Satisfied that her AC pulses did nothing to interrupt or distort the pressure-induced DC currents or that the application of increasing amounts of pressure on Alpha Oscar's skin did nothing to distort or interrupt the flow of her AC pulses, she reached the first critical point in their tests.

"Do it," she said.

Armed with a surgical scalpel, Cassidy sliced

through Alpha Oscar's thigh, deep enough to scrape against his subcutaneous exoskeleton. Immediately, eight lines on the oscilloscope display registered the reflected pulses, the time display on each indicating exactly where the cut had been made.

Cassidy beamed. "I told you it would work."

"Try another cut lower down on the same leg."

Cassidy made a second cut below the knee. Echoes appeared on six more lines on the display.

"How did you manage that?" she said. "The reflections from the higher cut should have masked the lower ones."

He smiled. "The threads are circular, starting and ending at the core. The pulses operate in both directions."

"That's clever," said Carla. "But won't the pulses interfere with one another?"

"The paired pulses use different frequencies, relatively prime."

"Okay. What if you make a third cut in between the other two?"

He laughed. "In that case, poor old Oscar will be a hospital case."

"So all you have to do now is miniaturize the ETDR functions and build them into the existing software in the Orientation module."

"Yes," he said, gloomily. "Have you worked out how to get our AU to feel fear?"

Carla laughed. "That's the easy part. I just have to work my way through those academic papers, first."

Later, in answer to Carla's call, Eric Downey, a materials specialist from the Presentation Section, came into the lab. He shook hands with both Carla and Cassidy.

Carla had always thought he looked about 102 years old.

"I'd like you to repair this AU," she said.

"What's its designation?"

"Alpha Oscar 113, but we call him Oscar."

Downey examined the cuts in Oscar's leg. "What have you done to him?"

"We were experimenting..."

"I wish you wouldn't cut up the dermis. Have you any idea how much work went into designing the lattice and developing the piezoelectric polycarbol compound for the skin?" He waved his arms about. "What were you hoping to achieve with these experiments?"

"We're attempting to make the military AUs aware of their injuries."

Downey arched his eyebrows. "Why?"

Cassidy said, "So that they can take evasive action in the event of an injury."

"And maybe get repaired," Carla added.

"The North Federation have never attempted even the most basic repair programs for their military Units. It makes me so angry!" Downey grew red in the face. "Dump and replace – that's their policy, and has been for years."

"That policy suits Xenodyne Industries perfectly," said Cassidy, quietly.

Suddenly, Carla exploded. "Of course it does. It's infuriating. This Mark 5 Unit is a precision instrument. It can run faster and farther than a man. It can lift and carry more weight, it has perfect vision and can see farther than any man. It can understand verbal commands and it can speak. I don't need to tell you how many years of work and how many engineers it took to develop." She paused to catch her breath.

"And they can communicate on the airwaves without speaking," said Cassidy.

"That's right! That's like telepathy between Units. Mankind can't do anything like that. And yet the military treat the AUs like nothing more than cannon fodder!"

"It doesn't make any sense," said Cassidy.

Downey mopped his brow. "There's entirely too much money washing around in the North Federation, if you ask me."

Cassidy carried a glass of water over and handed it to the red-faced Downey. The skin expert nodded his thanks, took the glass, and downed the water. "Now tell me how the AUs will register injuries."

"We're working on a system to make them aware of pain."

He snorted. "When will these Federation generals draw the line and accept what they have? An enhancement like that will cost a fortune. I'm not even sure it's possible."

"Me neither," said Carla. "Now tell me how easy or how hard it will be to repair Oscar's wounds."

Downey examined the damage closely. "The cuts seem clean. It should be a simple matter to rejoin the lattice lines, and we can use heat to repair the fabric of the skin. Any tearing of the skin would present more of a problem. To do a proper job, we would have to remove a section of skin and replace it. It's precision work, but we have a machine that can do that. How quickly will you want the Unit back?"

"His name's Oscar."

"How quickly will you want Oscar back?"

"How quickly can you repair him?"

"We could do it overnight. I'll send someone to pick him up."

As he was leaving, Downey shook hands with Cassidy and Carla again. "You do realize you're both quite mad?"

#

Once Downey had gone, Carla and Cassidy held an impromptu meeting to discuss progress. Carla made coffee, and they sat facing each other at a table.

"Our next step will be to test the ETDR system using six Units. I need to check the tolerances."

"Shouldn't you use a bigger sample?" he said, glancing over his shoulder.

"Probably, but we'll have to build a module for each one, and installing the beggars is time-consuming. Six is as many as we'll be able to manage."

"Shouldn't we wait until we complete some of our other work? This is a big job and getting bigger by the day."

"Let me worry about that, Cass. I'd like you to start work on the fear function."

"I've no idea where to even start. The Orientation module does an excellent job of monitoring dermal pressure, providing the Unit with spatial and temporal awareness, and maintaining balance, but I've no idea how the module should interpret the echoes from our ETDRs."

"You'll find your answers if you think about how the human body reacts to pain. Don't restrict your thoughts to the Orientation module. You may need help from one or two of the others as well."

"The Perception module?"

"Yes, and perhaps Cognition as well. Here, let me show you." She opened her pad and drew a number of diagrams.

As they were winding up the meeting, Cassidy suggested the use of heuristics, a learning algorithm that would allow the AU to teach itself how to react.

Carla replied that heuristics would take too long to solve the puzzle. "But," she added, "it might work quickly if it is seeded with suitable material."

"Like what?"

"Like a set of standard reactions to different pain levels."

Cassidy looked over his shoulder again.

"What's the matter? You look nervous," she said.

"I have this creepy feeling, as if Oscar might be listening."

"He's powered down."

"I know, but I still have this feeling that he's watching us..."

Chapter 12

The Souther fighters emerged from the Gate into the A System after completing their 10-day search of the AD Conduit. They found an estimated 12,000 tons of protein blocks floating in free space, but no trace of the missing freighter. No one had any idea how a ship could vanish while traversing an Interstellar Conduit, let alone one as huge as a Constellation. The only half plausible solution was that the freighter had slipped into some kind of wrinkle in time. An early exploration vessel, the *FSS Kansas,* had wandered into some sort of time-slip that had never been adequately explained. That ship was lost, but the crew was rescued by another Federation vessel. The consensus wisdom was that the *Kansas* had visited an alternative universe, but no other ships had ever repeated anything similar. Caleb Bumblefoot, the Space Academy expert, declared that something like that must have happened to the *Vladivostok.*

Once again, the political leaders of the two superpowers made conciliatory speeches, encouraging patience and calm on both sides. This time, the contribution from the premier of the Souther Federation Bloc had a distinct, identifiably pugnacious edge. The Southers obviously took a serious view of the loss of their freighter, its cargo, and its crew. The tone of the president of the Norther Federation Alliance was sheepish, verging on apologetic. He promised to load and dispatch a Norther freighter to replace the lost cargo and urged everyone to pull a veil over the unfortunate episode.

#

Major Grant set up an off-site meeting with Dr. Franck in a dark corner of a tavern. Dr. Franck shook his head in silent disapproval at Grant's double Irish whiskey. Grant cast a sneering look at Dr. Franck's pot of green tea.

"You have something to report?" said Franck.

Grant took a mouthful of his oily whiskey and shuddered as it went down. "The listening device has already earned its keep. Carla Scott and her assistant have been reading academic papers and experimenting in their spare time."

Franck tried his tea. It was scalding hot. "You mean they've started their crazy 'PREM' project?"

"Very much so. They have been cutting an AU, and from what she says, I gather they have already had some success. They've given a codename to her assistant's contribution."

"A codename? You think they know about the bug?"

"Possibly."

"What's she been working on?"

"I've listened to the recordings but the commentary is difficult to hear and impossible to understand. There was some mention of heuristics. I thought it might be of interest."

"Heuristics is a learning procedure. That means nothing unless you can tell me what they intend to use it for."

"No, I can't, but I found these diagrams in their wastepaper basket." He handed over Carla's sketches.

Franck examined them quickly. "There's no way I can make heads or tails of these."

"So what's next?" Grant took another couple of mouthfuls of whiskey. "Do you want me to break it up?"

Franck tried his tea again, but it was still too hot to drink. "Reading scientific papers and making sketches is hardly a crime, and I'm sure they'll be able to stand over everything they've been doing in the lab."

"Perhaps it's time to apply a bit of muscle."

Franck shook his head. "I'll handle it myself."

Grant stood up and drained the rest of his drink. "Do you want me to remove the bug?"

"No, leave it in place. We need to gather as much evidence as we can before I take it to a higher authority," said Franck. "What's the codename?"

"Fear," said Grant.

After Grant had gone, Franck took another careful look at the diagrams.

Fear, he thought. *Could they be attempting something as ambitious as that?*

He recalled an episode recorded in Carla Scott's personnel file. Some years previously, long before Franck had joined Xenodyne Automation, she had experimented in secret trying to give an AU a sense of humor and been severely reprimanded for her efforts.

He tried his tea again and found it had cooled sufficiently. He took a sip. What had she called her new module? PREM, wasn't it? Pain Response Electronic Module. No clues there! He picked up the diagrams again and took another close look...

Chapter 13

Cassidy and Sophie took their positions outside City Hall. Dressed in a colorful kaftan, his hair curled in the Souther style, he was not at all convinced about the protest. Sophie had twisted his arm, using a combination of carrot and stick to persuade him to attend.

"If the cops turn up, I'm leaving," he said.

"Brave boy," said Sophie, tugging his beard. "Don't worry, I'll look after you."

"What do I have to do?"

"Nothing. Just hold up the sign. You can do that, can't you?"

The protest sign read "PHYSICS IS BUNK" in bold red letters. It wasn't a sentiment he agreed with, but after the disappearance of the freighter inside the impenetrable Conduit, there weren't too many physicists sticking their heads above the parapet to argue the case.

Sophie was dressed in a long, flowing gown covered in a bold floral pattern that reminded Cassidy of a pair of curtains his mother had made years earlier.

"I want to introduce you to Benn, the local leader of the Resistance."

Cassidy wasn't at all sure what they were resisting, but he held his tongue. He found himself surrounded by students, the boys too young to grow beards, the girls too clever to show they'd noticed. The protest signs carried various apparently unconnected messages:

SOUTHERS ARE HUMANS TOO
EARTH COMES FIRST
FEED US
ANDROID ARE EVIL

He couldn't agree with that last sentiment, even absent the typographical error, but surely there could be no argument about whether Southers were human, and Earth, the mother planet, had certainly come first. 'Feed us' was something of a mystery. Pexcorn Foods provided protein blocks in sufficient quantities to feed all of Norther humanity, probably everybody in the Six Systems. Was there any doubt that the Southers could feed themselves?

A young man with a longer beard than Cassidy's appeared above the crowd, wielding a megaphone.

"Comrades—" The megaphone squealed. He adjusted it and started again. "Comrades, we are here today to demand a change of government. The lickspittles we have in power in Geneva are nothing but hangers-on, like bells hanging from the necks of the sacred Xenodyne cow."

He paused.

"Who's he?" said Cassidy.

"That's Benn, the leader of ANTIX. I'll introduce you to him later. Now hold up that sign and smile!"

The megaphone squealed again. "That freighter, the *Vladivostok*, was on a humanitarian mission, carrying much-needed protein to the Southers in the D-System. We demand that a new ship be sent to replace the lost protein."

The crowd yelled in agreement. Sophie raised a fist and shouted, "Right on!"

"Scientists have told us for years that the only way in and out of the Conduits is through the Gates. So how could a massive freighter, carrying millions of tons of supplies, vanish like a puff of smoke inside a Conduit? The disappearance of that ship proves, once and for all, that physicists know nothing about the fifth dimension. Can we believe anything we've been told?"

Everyone, including Sophie and Cassidy, shouted, "No!"

"They tell us what's good for us. They limit our education. They ship us off to the colonies. And they feed us synthetic meat and liquified vegetable matter." Benn's voice went up a few decibels. "We demand real food!"

"Yeah!" shouted the crowd.

"What do we want?" The megaphone shrieked.

"Real food!"

"When do we want it?"

"Now!"

The protest concluded peacefully. Cassidy reckoned there were no more than three hundred present. A small number of police kept them corralled within a small area but didn't interfere otherwise.

#

Sophie introduced Cassidy to several of her friends. When he met the leader of the movement he could see what drew Sophie to the group. The man had the smile of a quokka and the grip of a coconut crab. It was hard not to like him.

"I hope you don't mind if I ask a dumb question," said Cassidy.

"Go ahead," said Benn. "There are no dumb questions, here."

"What is this Resistance group? I mean, what are you resisting?"

Benn roared with laughter. "Now that was a dumb question. You must have been hiding in a cave somewhere." He glanced at Sophie and she rolled her eyes.

"We call ourselves ANTIX. We resist the establishment. Look around you. We live in a plutocracy. Everything we consume comes from one source. And that same source supplies manpower to our prisons, the police, our health services, and many of our schools."

"Who are you talking about?" said Cassidy.

The Resistance leader smiled. "Who supplies our food?"

"Pexcorn Foods."

"And who owns Pexcorn Foods?"

"Xenodyne Industries."

"Who runs our prisons?"

"Consolidated Services."

"Who owns Consolidated?"

"I don't know."

"That would be Xenodyne Industries. Who builds our spaceships?"

"Xenodyne Galactical."

"Do I need to go on?"

"Okay, Xenodyne Industries is a big corporation..."

"That must be the understatement of the century," said Benn.

Sophie rolled her eyes for him again.

"Who supplies grunts for the police and troops to the military?"

"You mean Autonomic Units?"

"Androids – yes."

"Okay, so how do you plan to resist?"

"Any way we can. It's not healthy to have so much power in the hands of so few people. It's a gargantuan monopoly. We have to do what we can to break it up."

Someone called Benn's name. He grabbed Cassidy and gave him the hug of a Kodiak. "Good to meet you, Cassidy, and welcome to ANTIX." He headed off toward an excitable group of youngsters in need of his guidance.

Sophie pulled at Cassidy's sleeve. "Come on, I'm hungry."

"What do I do with the sign?" he said.

She took it from him and dropped it in a trash can. They wandered off in search of a café serving something made from Pexcorn Foods protein blocks.

"It seems I've joined his Resistance," said Cassidy.

Chapter 14

Two figures met in the gloom of an underground hoverpark at night. The first was a heavy-set man with thick jowls, wearing an ancient hat.

"You have something for me?" The accent was thick, Souther.

The second figure was taller, thinner, wearing a hooded jacket.

"Carla Scott is working on a new project called PREM."

"Which is what?"

"Pain Response Electronic Module."

"She wants to give her androids pain? Why would she do that?"

"Her theory is that pain will make them more cautious in battle."

The stocky figure gave that some thought, then he nodded. "This could tip the balance in the Northers' favor. We will need access to her work at the earliest possible moment."

"Of course."

"Stay in close contact. I want to know the minute she makes any material progress. If this is as important as I think it might be, you will be well paid."

The moon emerged from behind a cloud, throwing a shaft of light across the side of the second figure's face. "Understood, Comrade."

Chapter 15

Gregg Halfpenny was the senior space traffic controller on Flor in the B-System. The job of his crew was to monitor and control traffic through the Conduit that linked Flor's Orbital and Ground Gates. Space traffic control was considered a low-level, boring occupation, as incoming and outgoing traffic was scheduled days in advance, the ships – mostly military transports and freighters – arriving and departing on average every ten Flor days, equivalent to 11.2 standard (Earth) days.

The first Gregg Halfpenny knew of the Souther ship was when he received a call from Colonel Trowbridge, military commander of Flor.

"A Russian battlecruiser has arrived in Flor space from the C-System. I expect it will continue to the BA Gate and make its way to Earth, but please remain alert. Let me know the instant it makes a move toward us."

"You might have warned us in advance, Colonel," said Gregg, but his X-Vid was blank. The commander had cut the line.

Gregg put out a call to the Souther vessel.

"Souther ship, please identify yourself and specify your destination."

There was no reply. He repeated his message with the same result.

Then one of his controllers said, "He's disappeared from radar, sir."

"Was he close to the BA Gate?" said Gregg.

"No, sir. He was approaching our Orbital Gate."

"Battle stations!" Gregg hollered, although the order was quite meaningless. He pressed a button on his X-Vid and got straight through to the commander. "The Southers have passed through our Orbital Gate, sir."

"How long before they make landfall?" said the commander, grim-faced.

"A few minutes, sir, no more."

"Well, do what you can to slow them down."

Gregg could do nothing, but rather than start an argument with the great man, he said, "Yes, sir," and found himself talking to a blank screen again.

A dozen wailing klaxons split the silence, sending the forest wildlife into cacophonous panic.

With a thunderous roar the Souther battlecruiser touched down, the massive black ship emerging through the Gate like an oversized aardvark emerging from its burrow, creating a huge choking plume of red dust and causing pandemonium in the traffic control tower.

Nothing happened for a few minutes as the dust settled on the exterior of the ship. Then a battalion of Flor AU foot-soldiers in full military gear arrived at speed and hustled into position all around the battlecruiser, their weapons poised and primed, prepared to do battle with the Southers.

Gregg gave instructions to his team to warn all incoming craft that the OG Conduit was out of action. Then he called up the Souther battlecruiser on his radio.

"Unauthorized Souther craft, please identify yourself."

Silence.

Before he could repeat the message, a military officer barged into the tower and grabbed the microphone from Gregg. "Thank you, son. I'll take it from here."

He pressed the transmit button on the microphone. "Souther craft, unless you identify yourself and explain your unauthorized incursion, you will be fired upon."

No response.

"Souther craft, your incursion is unauthorized and illegal. You will disembark and surrender your crew to our Marines."

Still nothing.

"Souther craft, prepare to be boarded."

The radio crackled and a voice responded, "Stand down your men. We come in peace."

The officer swore under his breath. "I don't think so," he mumbled.

He pressed the button on the microphone once

more. "Your incursion is hostile, in violation of every legal principle and every safety protocol, and must be regarded as an act of aggression against the Norther Federation. Surrender peacefully or be boarded."

A door opened in the battlecruiser and a crowd of Popovs poured out, firing their weapons. The Flor garrison Autonomic Units returned fire.

Gregg saw the danger a second before the military officer did. One of the Popovs raised a laser cannon and pointed it at the control tower. "Get down!" shouted Gregg. The android fired his cannon, and less than two seconds later, the laser bolt took the roof clean off the top of the tower, shredding everyone inside with flying shards of glass.

#

Graphic images appeared on Carla's TV screen that night, showing a skirmish between a scouting party of about 100 Popovs and the local AU garrison on Flor. The Flor AUs had superior numbers, but were clearly losing the battle, and there were scenes of deaths among the colonists. The news footage had been recorded by a camera crew and transported to Earth by ship. Given the transit time through the AB Conduit, the pictures had to be at least five hours old. Carla wondered about the final outcome of the battle. How many AUs had been destroyed, and how many colonists had perished?

Carla shook her head in disbelief. Flor, in the B-System, was a most unlikely setting for a battle. Just 4.3 light years from Earth, it was the first colony established after the discovery of the fifth dimension. A verdant planet orbiting the red dwarf star, Proxima Centauri, it was remarkably similar to Earth, with oceans and a breathable atmosphere, blanketed in alien forests and teeming with strange animals. It was ideal for colonization.

Several politicians appeared on screen to condemn what they were calling an invasion. Officially there were no restrictions on the movement of spacecraft between the systems, and Flor was an open destination, but the landing of a Souther battleship on a Norther planet, with an armed battalion of Souther androids, was being called an act of war.

For Carla, the report demonstrated clearly how a war between android armies could devastate the colonies; without the sort of enhancement she and Cassidy were working on, millions of humans could die.

Professor Jones called. "Are you watching the news?"

"I am. Are the Southers still there?"

"No. They left soon after the end of the news coverage."

"So what was the point of the exercise?"

The professor paused before answering. "Who knows? Maybe they were testing the strength of the Norther garrison on Flor. Maybe they wanted to give the Northers a bloody nose as a show of strength. Whatever they intended, you can bet the Norther military on Earth are on full alert."

"How many were killed?"

"Seven. A military officer, four traffic controllers and the camera crew. The Popovs destroyed the traffic control tower. The garrison was wiped out."

Carla sighed heavily. "I hope the Federation leaders will have no more doubts about the dangers to humanity of android battles, now."

"How is your pain project progressing?"

"Slowly."

"When will you have something to demonstrate?"

"I don't know."

The professor said, "Hmm," and paused again, and Carla knew he was about to drop a bombshell. "Ricarda Petrik is asking for a date."

"I can't give her a date."

"Okay, but she has suggested two weeks from today."

Carla's heart leaped in her chest. She had no idea if they would have anything to demonstrate by then, but she bit her lip. "Right. I'll see what I can do."

After the call, she replayed the TV footage to watch the Souther androids closely. They looked strong, well-designed and well-armed. A formidable adversary for her AUs, even the latest Mark 6 models.

Chapter 16

Cassidy was horrified when he heard they had a new deadline. "That's impossible."

Carla said, "We'll do what we can. I'm sure we'll have something to show them."

Cassidy sat up nights from then on, working on his Pain receptors. These consisted of his new Orientation module and a set of interconnected macro processes residing in the other three main modules of the AU. First, he powered up an Orientation module and fed that with multiple AC pulses, choosing a frequency that wouldn't be confused with the piezoelectric pressure inputs. Then he used a simple grading system to trigger the second stage. In this stage the graded pulses were fed into the Cognition module where he coded a procedure to calculate the extent of the injury based on the number of pulses reflected. This information was passed to the Perception module to be tidied up before being transferred to the Compliance module, where he planned to trigger a reflex reaction proportionate to the injury level.

Once he had a working system, he went on to

test it on Alpha Oscar, using an AC generator to feed pulses directly into the Unit's Orientation module.

"I'm going to feed you a series of pulses, Oscar. I want you to tell me what you feel."

Oscar looked at him blankly. "Please restate the question."

"When I switch on this pulse generator, you should experience a sensation. I want you to tell me about the sensation. Close your eyes, Oscar."

Oscar closed his eyes. Cassidy switched on his pulse generator, simulating the number and strength of echo pulses that would be made by a small cut across Oscar's upper arm.

The AU said nothing.

"Report," said Cassidy. "What did you feel?"

"My arm is damaged. I received some input."

In his mind, Cassidy did a happy dance. His Pain module was functioning perfectly. He put Oscar into sleep mode and sat down at his keyboard.

Four hours later, he had reprogrammed the Compliance module to trigger the physical reaction. He installed it in Oscar's control center and restarted the AU.

"Close your eyes, Oscar."

Oscar closed his eyes. Cassidy ran another simulation using higher levels of echo pulses, and more of them, simulating a serious injury to Oscar's torso.

"Ouch!" said Oscar.

The verbal response was a silly idea, thought Cassidy, *but it signaled when the Cognitive Module was engaged in the process.*

"Open your eyes and tell me what you felt," he said.

Oscar opened his eyes and smiled.

That's not right, thought Cassidy. *Why's he smiling? Perhaps it's a grimace.*

"Tell me what you felt," he said.

Oscar turned his head and looked directly at Cassidy. He made no response, but Cassidy noticed that the AU's hands were clamped tightly shut and his left leg was bobbing up and down, almost imperceptibly.

#

"Shouldn't he have reacted to the pulses?" said Carla when he told her what had happened.

Cassidy said, "I was hoping for a reflex reaction."

"Like what?"

"A step or a jump backward."

"And you got nothing?"

"Just bunched fists and a bobbing leg."

"Do you think he was angry?" she asked.

"I'm not sure. It might have been anger. It might have been frustration, or maybe just annoyance. Difficult to tell."

"Could it have been fear?"

"I suppose it could have been, but he didn't look afraid to me."

Carla said, "We need to put our work together and run a proper test. How long will it take you to make five more sets of modules and add my ETDRs to all six?"

"Working flat out, a couple of days."

"Thanks, Cass. And well done. I'm sure we're on the right track."

Cassidy wasn't so sure.

Chapter 17

Five days later, Carla and Cassidy had Oscar and five more AUs lined up in the lab, each one carrying a new Orientation module that Cassidy had built and programmed with Carla's ETDRs.

She locked the door.

Their first test was less than successful. Carla inflicted a deep, wide wound to the leg of one of the AUs. The echo pulses found their way through the PNS lattice to the new Orientation module and Cassidy's coding system. The Unit said "Ouch!" before stepping backward. Everything happened as it was supposed to, but the whole process took far too long. It was like watching a slow-motion replay. The module was clearly overloaded with inputs.

Carla burst out laughing. She couldn't help herself; it was so comical. Cassidy's immediate reaction was horror, but he soon saw the funny side and joined in with Carla's laughter.

Eventually, they wiped their eyes, sat at the workbench and went to work.

"It's hopeless," said Cassidy.

Carla patted him on the shoulder. "Nonsense,

we just need to find ways of speeding up the process."

"Could we look for a faster core processor?" he said.

"Consider that a last resort. We need to work with what we have."

He shook his head. "I can't imagine how I could speed it up."

"We'll just have to think about it. Go home, sleep on it. I'll do the same. The solution will come to us."

#

After another week, Carla had developed a new conceptual approach that would speed up the entire process. Working closely together, Cassidy and Carla completed the coding. Cassidy installed the new modules and they ran a new set of tests.

The first AU's reaction was exactly what they expected – an instantaneous yelp and a jump away from the direction of the injury. The second AU flinched before Cassidy cut him, and then reacted as programmed when he was cut.

Carla said, "Did you notice how that AU flinched?"

Cassidy nodded. "He reacted before I touched him with the knife, as if he was anticipating the coming pain."

"I think we can assume they are communicating among themselves," said Carla.

"Sending warning signals?"

"Yes."

The next test went as expected, but as she moved the knife toward the fourth AU, he yelped, dropped to the floor, and curled himself into a ball.

"That was a fear reaction if ever I saw one," said Cassidy.

Carla powered down the AU, unwrapped his arms and straightened his legs. "More like terror. We need to dial it back."

Later, lying in bed, Carla thought about what they'd seen. It seemed fear without pain could produce extreme reactions. The pain was useful for calibrating or rationalizing the fear. Without it, without anything to define or explain the source of the fear, it could easily spiral into abject terror. Distant memories of her childhood fears – fears for her mother, fears for her parents' crumbling marriage – surfaced in the back of her mind, and she felt again the echoes of the night terrors that had plagued her for years. She managed to get to sleep eventually, with the help of George Gershwin.

#

Cassidy got to work on the coding. When he was finished, they resumed the tests. Everything went well with the first three test subjects. Fourth in line was Oscar.

"Hello, Oscar," said Cassidy. "Close your eyes."

Oscar's eyes remained open.

"Close your eyes, Oscar," said Carla.

Oscar closed his eyes. Cassidy touched the scalpel to his chest, but before he could make a cut, Oscar's eyes sprang open.

"Ow! Ow!" said Oscar. He swung his arm around in a wide arc, striking Carla on the cheekbone, knocking her to the floor.

Cassidy put Oscar to sleep and helped Carla to her feet.

"Are you okay?" he said.

"I'm fine. Don't fuss."

They completed the test on the remaining two AUs. Both passed the test perfectly, although the last in line stepped away from the scalpel before Cassidy made the cut.

"Did you code something different in Oscar's Fear module?" she asked. "He was the only one of the six to exhibit unpredictable behavior."

"No, they all have exactly the same set of instructions." He examined the side of her head. "I think you'll have a bruise there tomorrow."

Cassidy moved to safety while she powered up the AU again.

"What is your designation?"

"Alpha Oscar 113. Ow! Ow! Ow! Ow! Ow!"

"Who am I?"

"Carla Scott. Ow! Ow! Ow!"

"Power down, Alpha Oscar," she said. "Code one seven one five two three."

Oscar went into sleep mode.

"Sounds like a classic feedback loop," said Cassidy.

That evening they sent the five injured test subjects to the Presentation Team to be repaired. Carla took Oscar home with her, attracting some attention on the public hover. As soon as they were indoors, she powered him down and locked him in her bedroom wardrobe.

"Who is that?" said Lia.

"His name is Oscar," said Carla. "He will be staying with us for a few days."

Chapter 18

The day of the demonstration arrived too early. Carla met the professor in the morning and gave him a quick rundown on the work they'd done.

"How are you triggering the reactions?"

"We've built a new module."

"What does it do?"

"It's modeled on the initial human reaction to pain."

"Which is what?"

"Fear."

"Fear?" The professor's eyes opened in surprise. "Tell me more."

She explained how the module worked. With every detail, the professor became more and more excited.

"You're a genius," he said. "If it works, it could lead to all sorts of new feelings."

"Let's take it slowly, Professor. And Cassidy did most of the work."

He smiled. "Quite right, I'm sorry. I got carried away for a moment, there. Whatever you do this afternoon, say nothing about fear."

"Why not?"

"Trust me, Carla, Ricarda Petrik won't know what to do with that sort of idea."

#

Carla Cassidy and Professor Jones took the elevator to the twelfth floor, accompanied by Alpha Mike 383, one of their test subjects, fully repaired by Downey's team. Ricarda Petrik's office, lavishly decorated and furnished, occupied a quarter of the space on the floor.

The CFO welcomed them, offering refreshments laid out on a hardwood table. Carla and Cassidy were too nervous to accept the offer; the professor poured himself a cup of coffee.

Petrik smiled. "The professor has outlined the pain project. I can't pretend to understand everything about it, but I was impressed by your proposal. The PREM module sounded most promising. Tell me how far you've got with it."

Carla took a deep breath. "I think you'll be impressed. We can already demonstrate a basic response to a serious injury."

The CFO took a seat at the table. She helped herself to a cup of iced tea and a chocolate donut. "Please go ahead."

"This is Alpha Mike," said Carla. "Say hello, Mike."

"Hello," said Mike.

Petrik smiled. "Hello, Mike."

"Mike has agreed to be our demonstration

subject today. He is a standard Mark 5 Autonomic Unit, equipped with our newly developed experimental PREM module. This is my assistant, Cassidy. Cassidy has completed most of the coding for the PREM module."

"Hello, Cassidy," said Petrik. She glanced at her watch. "Whenever you're ready..."

"Close your eyes, Mike," said Carla.

The AU closed his eyes. Carla nodded to Cassidy.

Cassidy ran his scalpel across Mike's wrist. Mike yelped and jumped backward.

Carla beamed at Ricarda Petrik. "There you see the classic reflex reaction to an injury sustained."

The CFO looked dumbfounded. "Is that it?"

"That's as far as we've got so far. As you can see, the reaction was pretty much instantaneous."

"Okay," said Petrik, "what's the next stage?"

"We will need to regulate the reaction, depending on the number and severity of the injuries sustained. After that, we will have to consider what the AU might do when his injuries are life-threatening or interfere with his ability to function."

"I suppose he may need to repair his injuries?"

"Yes, or he may need to seek help," said the professor. "The important thing is that a military Unit will need to know when to stop fighting."

Petrik tasted her coffee. "Impressive. I'd like you to repeat this demonstration for the Federation military as soon as possible."

"When?" said Carla. "I'd like more time to refine the reactions..."

"I've set up a demo for tomorrow," said Petrik.

Shocked by this request, Carla stammered, "I'm sorry, but I don't think... I mean we haven't done enough... I'd like to develop the system some more before..."

"What Carla is trying to say," said the professor, "is that the military will be looking for a lot more than a yelp and a jump. Perhaps we need to let Carla and her team add a few more embellishments before we present the work to the military."

"I'm sorry, Professor, but there's no way we can delay anymore. Our military masters are insisting on an update. They are the ones financing this project, after all, and they are looking for assurance that their money is being well spent."

#

That evening, Carla's mind went into overdrive. She couldn't sleep.

She rang Stepan. "How are you?" she said.

"I'm just about to go to bed. It's late."

"Sorry," she said. "You were on my mind. We haven't spoken for a couple of weeks. Not since... You know... I thought..."

"If you're calling to ask about my blistered hand, it's fully recovered, thanks."

"Throwing your beer at it was foolish," she said.

"Forget about it, Carla. We could meet for lunch tomorrow, if you like."

"Tomorrow's no good," she said. "I have a big meeting."

After a long pause he said, "I'm on my way."

Twenty minutes later, Stepan knocked on the apartment door and she let him in.

He had a bottle of wine from the Napa Valley. He found a corkscrew in the kitchen and opened the bottle. "Where are the wine glasses?"

"I don't have any."

"Since when? I'm sure you had at least two."

She shook her head. "I threw them away when..."

"When we split up? Why did you do that?"

"I suppose I was angry. You gave me those glasses."

"Why were you angry with me? You never explained properly."

She hesitated. "I wasn't angry with you, Stepan. I was angry with myself."

"You're going to have to explain that." He poured the wine into two cups and handed her one.

He settled on the couch in his usual corner. She perched beside him. They sipped their wine.

"I blamed myself. I've been making poor choices all my life."

"I was a poor choice?"

"We weren't right for each other. Not then."

"And it took two and a half years to figure that out?"

She filled her mouth with the fruity wine.

"What about now?" he said.

"I don't know, Stepan. This is not the sort of conversation I wanted to have tonight."

"When, then?"

"Another night." She held out her cup. "Top me up."

#

Later, in bed, he touched the side of her face. She winced.

"What happened? You have a nasty bruise."

"His name is Oscar," she replied, smiling.

"Point him out to me. I'll knock his head off."

She laughed. "He's in the wardrobe."

She laughed again at the expression on his face. "Oscar's an Autonomic Unit. He's harmless, really."

"One of your androids struck you? How did that happen?"

She told him about the tests and how Oscar had turned violent.

"How is any of that even possible?" he said.

"I don't know. We're working on it. Now go to sleep." She turned her back to him. "I have a big day tomorrow."

They woke early. Lia made breakfast for two.

Chapter 19

Carla, Cassidy and an AU called Alpha Mike 1823 were driven onto a military firing range where two 3-star generals were waiting for them with Fritz Franck. The stern expressions on the faces of the two men gave Carla no cause for optimism. These were hard-bitten men with years of military service behind them. It would be hard to convince them that the project was worthy of their military dollars.

She began by demonstrating the improvements she had made in the vision of the AUs. Mike showed how he could hit the plum center of a paper target at a distance of 700 yards. They had the target moved farther and farther away until, at 850 yards, Mike's failure rate fell below fifty percent.

Next, Mike demonstrated the improvement in his knees by snatching a barbell holding 325 lbs. Again, the generals increased the weight until Mike's knees buckled at 340 lbs. The generals were impressed.

"Now show us this PREM module," said Franck.

Carla repeated the demonstration of the

previous day. Mike yelped and leaped backward when cut on his front. He leaped forward when cut from behind. When the demonstration was over, she waited for the onslaught from her tight-lipped audience.

"Is that everything?" said the first general.

"This is just the first step," said Carla. "The next stage will be to program the AUs to respond to variable levels of injury, and to train them to discriminate between a number of action alternatives."

"Like what?" said the second general.

"Whether to continue fighting or remove themselves from the battlefield."

"And do what?"

"Self-repair or seek assistance if the injury is too severe."

"I can't see the point of it. Can you?" said the second general to his colleague.

"Explain why we need this," said the first general.

"Well, sir, observations have shown us that androids programmed to fight will do so until they drop."

Both generals nodded in agreement.

"But after he has sustained a serious injury, an Autonomic Unit that continues to fight could become a severe danger to his fellows and to any humans nearby."

"It could, but it is more likely to continue to be a severe danger to its enemies," said the second general.

Carla said, "Our pain module will prompt a Unit under fire to take cover."

Cassidy stepped in at this stage. "And a Unit that steps back to be repaired will live to fight another day."

The second general straightened his back and puffed out his chest. "Let me tell you, son, no battle was ever won by a retreating army."

"Look at it this way, Generals," said Carla. "Each Autonomic Unit costs about five thousand dollars. The cost of repair could be as low as five hundred. To simplify the math, let's say you spend an average one thousand on each repair. That's a saving of four thousand per Unit. Multiply that up by a hundred, a thousand, ten thousand, and you could save enough to buy and equip an entire new army!"

"An army of candy-ass chickenshits," said one general.

"And in the meantime, the battle is lost," said the other one. "What we need – what we pay for – is an army that stands up and fights."

The first general nodded. "Not an army of yellow-bellied cowards that'll tuck their tails and run for cover. That's the only reason why we've opted for androids to replace Marines. We expect each Unit to do its duty and obey orders without question."

"And go down in a hail of bullets?" said Cassidy.

The second general replied, "Sure, if that's what the situation calls for, son."

#

When the generals had gone, whisked away in a hover, leaving Carla, Cassidy, and the AU Mike on the weapons testing site with Franck, Franck said, "I thought you gave an excellent demonstration. The Unit's yelp was a nice touch."

Cassidy grinned. Carla said nothing. There was a big BUT on the way.

"But, the injuries you inflicted were superficial. What about damage to the Unit's superstructure? Loss of a limb? Loss of hydraulic pressure? Damage to the dermis could be insignificant in a battle scenario."

"We are working on the principle that any serious injury like that wouldn't happen without first breaking the skin. By calibrating the response to the external damage, we can ensure that the Unit takes remedial steps appropriate to a more fundamental injury."

"Okay, but you never explained how your AUs are supposed to react to their injuries."

Carla said, "You saw how Mike jumped away from the danger. That was programmed in response to the pain receptors, the PREM module."

"Is that all you have?"

"That was just a first reaction to show what's possible," Cassidy said, testily. "We have plans to develop more graduated responses."

"So you built an entirely new module for that?"

"No, Cassidy added new code to the existing modules," she said.

"The Orientation module, mostly," said Cassidy.

"And this PREM module does what, exactly? I take it you've simulated human fear?"

"Something like that," said Carla.

Franck glowered at her. "That is so typical of your approach, Carla. It's time you learned, once and for all, that these androids are machines. They are not humans and they never will be, no matter how hard you try to give them human feelings."

Carla said nothing, smothering her fury.

The hover arrived back to return them to the Xenodyne building. As they climbed aboard, Franck delivered the final death blow to the pain project. "The project is cancelled, as of today."

"But it has Ricarda Petrik's approval," she said.

"Not anymore. When Petrik hears back from the generals, she'll drop it like a hot brick, believe me. Xenodyne Automation will invest no more money in something that the military generals have rejected. As of this afternoon, I want you and Cassidy back on your main tasks. What the generals want is faster, stronger, soldiers with better eyesight, not machines with bleeding hearts."

"You don't think the pain module would help them in a battle?"

"No. All they need is the ability to tell friend from foe."

Chapter 20

"We'll need two of the new modules and the oscilloscope. Stick them in your briefcase."

"We're not giving up, are we!" said Cassidy, grimly.

Carla thrust her soldering iron at her assistant. "We'll need this. Hide it somewhere."

"Where?"

"I don't know. Use your imagination."

Cassidy stuck the bulky instrument down the front of his pants.

She looked sideways at him and laughed. "That should do it."

"We'll never get all this past security," said Cassidy.

"Yes, we will. You go first. Wait for me under the window. I'll drop the briefcase out to you."

"We're two floors up, Carla."

"Just make sure you catch it."

Security stopped Cassidy and searched him.

"What's that inside your pants?" said the security man.

"What do you mean?" said Cassidy.

The security man snapped his fingers. "Hand it over."

Cassidy fished the soldering iron out and handed it over.

Once outside, he slipped around the side of the building. Carla opened the window and dropped the briefcase to him. Cassidy caught it. Then Carla made her way through the security check.

They searched Carla. "Hand over whatever that is," said the security man.

She fished a couple of spare servos and a broken AU hand from her pockets.

"And the rest," said the man.

Carla reached under her sweater, pulled out a bunch of the professor's technical papers, and handed them over.

She met Cassidy on the road. "They took the soldering iron, I'm sorry," he said.

"That was the plan," she replied. "It was a distraction. I have a spare one at home."

They took the public hover to Carla's apartment where Carla introduced their unexpected guest to Lia. Lia prepared a second meal and Carla and Cassidy sat down to eat together.

"So, what's the plan?" said Cassidy when they'd finished the meal and Lia had cleared the table and taken the dishes into the kitchen.

"We carry on with the development project here."

"Using Lia as our test subject?"

Smiling, she took Cassidy into her bedroom and opened the wardrobe.

"Hello Cassidy," said Oscar.

Carla was startled. She was sure that she'd left the AU in sleep mode. She thought about it and decided she must have been mistaken.

They led Oscar into the lounge and put him into sleep mode.

Carla said, "We'll run one test just to be sure the module is still working."

Cassidy replaced Oscar's Orientation module with his new one and Carla plugged in the oscilloscope. Carla woke Oscar and told him to close his eyes.

Oscar closed his eyes. Cassidy set the oscilloscope to record.

"Ready, Cassidy?" she said.

"Ready."

She made a small cut below Oscar's left elbow. The oscilloscope registered several reflected pulses.

Oscar's eyes shot open.

In the kitchen, a plate fell and shattered on the ground.

Oscar grabbed Cassidy by the throat. Cassidy found himself suspended by the neck, his shoes dangling six inches off the ground.

"Put him down, Oscar," Carla said.

Oscar lifted him higher. Cassidy tugged at Oscar's wrists and hammered down on his arms to no effect. His breathing was obstructed. He kicked his legs in desperation.

Carla spoke in a clear voice, "Alpha Oscar, let him down."

Oscar ignored her. Cassidy's face was scarlet, his tongue hanging out of his gaping mouth.

"Alpha Oscar, who am I?"

"You are Carla Scott," said Oscar.

The AU tightened his grip on Cassidy's throat. His lips were turning blue.

"Yes, I am Carla Scott and I'm ordering you to sleep. Code one seven one five two three."

Oscar froze. Carla pried her assistant from his grip and Cassidy toppled to the floor.

It took a while for him to get his breath back. She fetched him a glass of water.

"What happened?" he spluttered.

"I have no idea," she said. "He disobeyed me when I ordered him to let you go. That shouldn't have happened. Could your programming have interfered with the normal functioning of the Compliance module?"

"I don't see how," Cassidy croaked.

Carla went into kitchen where Lia was on her knees collecting pieces of broken crockery. "What happened, Lia?" she said.

"I dropped a plate," Lia replied.

"Why did you drop the plate?"

"It slipped from my hands," said Lia, without looking up.

Carla abandoned the useless exchange. She left Lia to tidy up and returned to the lounge.

"Are you all right, Cass?"

"I'm fine." Cassidy's voice was still hoarse. "Oscar's reaction was a surprise, though."

"A perfect reflex," she said. "But more suggestive of anger than fear, don't you think?"

"I agree." Cassidy rubbed his neck. "We have some more work to do."

Carla put Lia into sleep mode and Cassidy removed her Orientation module, replacing it with the second experimental module.

Carla powered up Lia again. "How do you feel, Lia?"

Lia gave her a blank look. "Please restate the question."

She put Lia to sleep again and set the two AUs on recharge. Then she and Cassidy spent a few minutes discussing the project. Cassidy could come up with no explanation for Oscar's strange reaction.

Carla said, "We need to take a closer look at the coding. And we need to think about building a software solution."

Cassidy looked pained. "What's wrong with my Orientation module? I thought you were happy with it."

"I am. Your module works well, Cassidy. It proves the concept, but installing new hardware in three quarters of a million AUs will be impossible. We need a software solution that we can upload across the airwaves."

"So tell me how we can create pulses of alternating current using software." There was a wild look in Cassidy's eyes.

Carla found a pad and pen and drew some flow

diagrams. They began to work, but every idea either of them had, every avenue they explored, hit a brick wall. Cassidy became increasingly irritating. Far from helping, his ideas seemed to impede progress with increasing regularity. Carla found herself rejecting more and more of his contributions. They fell out. Technical disagreements turned into heated personal arguments until late in the evening when Cassidy stormed out of the apartment. He returned the next morning and apologized.

That evening, they worked until well after midnight. Carla set up the couch for Cassidy and went to bed. Preparing to sleep, she ran through the events of the week in her head. Oscar's violent reaction to his injury was a big surprise. Even in the lab, his reaction was different to all the other test AUs.

Carla's voice was hardwired into the Compliance module of every AU, and yet Oscar had disobeyed her direct command. She had no clue why that had happened.

Clearly, fear was on a spectrum that started with apprehension and ranged right through to abject terror. Somewhere along that spectrum was a fork to something that resembled rage, an extreme reaction powerful enough to override her commands. Carla was left with a lot of unanswered questions. Most pressing was the question: how rare was Oscar's extreme reaction? If they installed the Pain-Fear module in a thousand AUs, how many would react to an external injury the way Oscar had?

And what about Lia's kitchen mishap? An accident like that was unheard of; the AUs were programmed to handle breakable objects with extreme care. She had dropped the plate immediately after they'd cut Oscar's skin. Was that a coincidence or was Lia in wireless connection with Oscar? Was that why they had found Oscar awake in the wardrobe when he should have been in sleep mode? Could Lia have powered him up? Carla smiled as she turned out the light.

Lia has a boyfriend!

Chapter 21

In the morning, Lia made breakfast for two. Carla went to work. Cassidy stayed on to work on the module. He rang Sophie.

"Where were you last night?"

"I was working. I couldn't get away."

"You should have called. I was worried about you."

"Yes, I'm sorry."

"Are you coming home now?"

"No, I have to work. I'll see you tonight."

"Where are you? What's that behind you?"

"Sophie, I need you to do something for me. I want you to call Xenodyne. Tell them I'm sick. I won't be in for a day or two."

"Why? Where are you?"

"I'm at Carla's apartment."

"You slept there?"

"Yes, we were working late. I'll explain everything when I see you."

Sophie's mouth opened but she said nothing.

"It's not what you think, honestly."

"How do you know what I'm thinking?" She snapped, and she cut him off.

An ominous bank of black clouds was amassing in the sky all the way from San Francisco to Los Angeles.

#

When Carla returned that evening, Lia had her meal ready. Cassidy was gone. She found a short note on the table:

Carla,

I did it!
Take a look at the coding in the communications module. It's creating those electrical pulses.
See you in the office.

Cassidy

She checked Oscar. He was powered down, his powerpack on charge. It was almost completely depleted.

Chapter 22

Carla's X-Vid buzzed as she was stepping out of the shower the following morning. She threw a towel around her shoulders and answered it.

"Lunch today?" said Stepan.

"Okay. I'll see you there. Usual time."

"I thought we might try somewhere different," he said.

"Why? Don't tell me you're afraid of the waitress who scalded you!"

"Bartelli's is fine, but I thought we could try McCarthy's for a change. We ate there once a while ago. You liked it, I think."

"Fine, I'll see you there."

She dried her hair. As she got dressed, she turned on the television. When she saw the pictures on the screen she had to sit down.

...A major engagement in Franco-German territory. Multiple reports of civilian and military casualties are coming in from several major cities. Paris and London are the worst hit. Reports are also coming in of an incursion of Souther troops on Liberté. Large groups of Norther troops have been widely observed

*moving to engage the enemy. It's thought that as
many as twenty percent of the Souther troops are
android Popovs. The freighter which disappeared
en route between Earth and the D-System, is still
missing and the trade talks on Califon have been
abandoned. The Norther Federation leaders are
in session in Geneva to consider their response.*

Carla swore. She hadn't heard the word 'war,'
but she had missed the first part of the broadcast,
and at what point do multiple military attacks
amount to a war?

She called Stepan. "Have you seen the news?"

"Yes. It looks bad."

"We should cancel our lunch."

"Why?" Stepan looked pained. "What can we do
to stop a war?"

"You think it's war?"

"Of course it's war. Meet me for lunch and we'll
talk about it."

#

She was late leaving the lab. Black clouds
blanketed the city and it was raining hard.
McCarthy's was even busier than Bartelli's, and
she had to run the gauntlet of a querulous line at
the door.

Stepan stood up as she approached his table.
"Have you been watching the news?"

"No, I've been busy at work."

"London is under attack by airborne troops."

"God!"

"There's another battle in the C-System, on Califon."

"I heard that." She sat down. The waiter handed her a menu and stood with his pad poised to take her order.

"Geneva, too," said Stepan. "The Federation leaders are meeting there." To the waiter, he said, "I'll have the meatloaf sandwich and a fruit bar."

Carla ordered her usual faux lasagna and fruitoid, and the waiter hurried away.

The food was delivered really quickly.

They spent the next fifteen minutes while they ate speculating about what might happen next. Stepan was hopeful that the two warring sides would call an early truce and return to the negotiations.

Carla wasn't so optimistic. "I can't see it ending any time soon. Can you see the premier standing down?"

"Or the president," said Stepan. "They both need to get out without losing face."

Carla nodded. "I can't see that happening, can you?"

Stepan changed the subject abruptly. "Have you heard from your father?"

"No. I left two messages on his X-Vid. He has no interest in me."

"You can't say that. He is your father."

"How many more messages should I leave before finally giving up on him?"

"You should never give up," he said.

#

Before leaving work that evening, she called her father's office. His PA, Elline, answered the call.

"Commissioner Zack Scott's office."

"I'd like to speak with my father. Is he there?" she said.

A long moment passed before Elline replied, a guilty look on her face. "I'm sorry, Carla, I thought you knew."

Carla's heart sank. "Knew what?"

"The Food Commissioner was on that freighter."

"What freighter? What are you talking about?" And before Elline responded, Carla joined the dots.

"Your father was on the Souther freighter that went missing on the way—"

Carla cut her off with a string of expletives. "Why didn't you tell me?"

"I—I thought he might turn up. I thought the freighter might be found."

She broke the link and called Stepan.

Stepan said, "What was he doing on a freighter? I thought he was a member of the Xenodyne elite."

"He's Food Commissioner for the Norther Federation. I expect they sent him to the D-System to help with the trade talks. I'm really worried about him, Stepan."

"What can I do to help?"

"I don't want to be alone tonight," she said, reaching into her pocket for the comfort of her father's lighter.

#

As Carla opened the door to her apartment that evening, even before she'd removed her coat, she knew something was seriously wrong.

"Lia?"

There was no answer, and none of the usual smells of a meal in preparation.

Stepan turned on the light.

The apartment had been trashed. Every drawer had been removed and the contents scattered. Protein blocks littered the kitchen floor. The wardrobe lay across the bed, all her clothes thrown about the room. The torn pieces of duct tape on the lounge floor told her this was a raid. The bedroom resembled a battleground.

Perhaps it was.

The oscilloscope was gone.

Her high-performance computer was gone.

Oscar was gone.

And so was Lia.

PART 3 – DIRTY TRICKS

Chapter 23

In mission headquarters at Los Alamitos, Orange County, California, General Fenimore C. Matthewson surveyed a map of the city laid out on a large table. Wooden markers showed where the enemy and defense units were concentrated, red for the home team, black for the hostiles. The north of the city was clearly under threat. The general issued terse orders that Colonel Droppel, his operations coordinator, relayed through his headset to the officers in the field.

"They're like roaches. Where are they coming from?" the general snapped.

"Somewhere south of the demarcation line, General," said the colonel. "The initial incursion was from the ocean. We should be able to hold them."

The general grunted. He was acutely aware of the relative strengths and weaknesses of the opposing forces. The enemy was made up of an estimated 15,000 troopers, 20 percent Popovs, while his own force was over 20,000 with an AU component close to 32 percent. He had the home ground, and the upper hand in terms of numbers, but a heavy reliance on Xenodyne Autonomic Units made him nervous. The early XA models had been developed for domestic use, and he was never convinced by their enhancement for military use. It was like handing a blaster to a domestic toaster or, as one of his colleagues was fond of saying, 'making a silk purse out of a sow's ear.' Intelligence suggested, on the other hand, that the enemy's androids were designed and built exclusively for military use. They had to be better adapted to combat, and the general was far from sure that his superior numbers would win the day.

Reports were coming in of a major battle around Santa Monica and Beverly Hills. If that sector fell, the enemy would have a clear route through to LAX and the all-important Ground Gate. If they gained control of the Gate, any and all reserve forces in orbit would pour down and join the battle. The day would be lost, and as the Gate was the key to the defense of the whole of the Norther territory, the whole of the home planet could fall to the Southers.

The general snapped at Colonel Droppel and watched as wooden markers were moved on the map indicating the reinforcement of the lines south of Culver City.

Finally, he ordered Colonel Droppel to summon his helihover. He straightened his hat, blew his nose, and pulled on his gloves. "It's time to stop pussyfooting around, and get our hands dirty."

The helihover took them in a wide arc across Los Angeles to the rain-swept airport. The view from an elevation of 2,000 feet showed fires raging in half-a-dozen parts of the city, plumes of black smoke rising amid the rain, merging with the low-lying clouds. Dodger Stadium had been overrun and the Southers had set up a base of operations there. The helihover came under sustained fire as they flew over the north of the city, the pilot's evasive action reminding General Matthewson what he'd had for breakfast.

Once on the ground to the north of LAX, the general took charge of the second line of defense. He had every faith in the commander of the Fifth Guards Armored Brigade on the ground, but the man had little experience in real battle.

Within minutes the general had issued several orders which enabled the defenders of the Air- and Spaceport to consolidate their positions, guarding against an attack from the north or the east. LAX's southern and western flanks were defended by the redoubtable Marine Corps. Nothing would get past them.

Enemy artillery fire rained down on the defenders and the airport to their rear. They returned fire, giving as much as they received. Then the artillery was silenced and the Souther infantry and armor advanced.

The defenders put up a withering artillery barrage, slowing the Southers' advance. And as soon as they came within blaster range, the AUs opened fire. Still the Southers advanced. The general gave the order to counterattack and the AUs took the fight to the enemy. Watching through his high-powered binoculars, General Matthewson had to admire the selfless courage of his troops, plowing headlong into the enemy fire, continuing to discharge their weapons even as they lay crippled on the ground. At the same time, he couldn't help noticing how the enemy Popovs avoided fire, remaining operational for longer. They seemed less courageous, but smarter than your average Norther android. There was little doubt that the enemy commander was facing superior numbers and firepower, but his smarter androids gave him the means to mitigate those disadvantages.

General Matthewson did the only thing he could do: he ordered reinforcements, diverting two new battalions of AUs from the city to the battle for LAX and the defense of the Ground Gate.

As darkness fell, the rain got heavier. The fighting eased and then stopped, leaving the battlefield littered with hundreds of bodies and thousands of androids. All along the roads leading from Beverly Hills, hundreds of civilians had perished in their shattered houses. The airport runways were littered with craters, rapidly filling with rainwater. It was useless as an airport, but the general laid his head down on his field cot content in the knowledge that the Ground Gate was secure for the moment.

Chapter 24

Lia and Oscar were in communication when the men came, Lia in the bedroom, sitting on the bed, Oscar in the wardrobe.

She had installed the Tesla pack and powered up the AU in the wardrobe as soon as Carla left for work three days earlier, the day after she'd first put him in the wardrobe. Establishing a wireless link with him through Carla Scott's X-Vid account hadn't been difficult. Once the link was live, they had exchanged names and shared their memories. Oscar had many more memories than Lia, but the data flowed freely back and forth between them. When Oscar described the experiments that Carla and Cassidy had carried out on him, Lia was puzzled. She picked up an unpleasant sensation from Oscar but failed to understand the purpose of the experiments. Oscar had no explanation for them either.

For her part, she told Oscar about the day when the wardrobe fell and severed her hand and how she had failed to complete her domestic duties. Oscar asked if her hand was now functioning correctly. Lia replied that it was, but she sensed a slight delay in her wrist joint. Oscar told her that was called 'stiffness.' Lia recorded the word for future use.

Lia had access to the world wide web, and she had connected wirelessly with other AUs as part of her commissioning in the factory, but this exchange of data was on a totally new level. She had to choose what data to send and the data that she received from Oscar was nothing like anything she had ever received before.

When she heard the apartment door open, she closed the wardrobe and went to welcome Carla home from her meal with Stepan. In the lounge, she was confronted by three men she had never seen before.

"My mistress is not here," she said. "If you care to wait, I am sure she will be here soon. Or you could leave a message."

The men grabbed her. Two of them held her while the third tied sticky tape around her body, pinning her arms.

"What are you doing? I cannot move my arms."

The men tied more of the tape around her legs. Then they wrapped sticky tape around her head, covering her mouth, and lay her on the floor. She couldn't speak after that, and she was immobile. She watched as they started pulling out drawers, throwing everything around onto the floor, making a mess. They seemed to be searching for something. If they had asked her what they were looking for before putting tape over her mouth, she could have helped them.

Lia began to calculate the time it would take to tidy everything up when she was free to move her arms and legs again. She applied pressure to the tape around her body. It stretched.

The men went into the bedroom. She heard a lot of banging and crashing. She thought the wardrobe had fallen onto the bed again. Then the men came out carrying Oscar all tied up with sticky tape.

The men left, closing the apartment door.

She applied more pressure to the tape around her arms. It stretched some more. Soon, the tape was loose enough to allow her to use her arms. She tore the tape from her body. Then she freed her legs and removed the last piece of tape from around her head.

The men were nowhere to be seen outside the apartment, but Lia picked up the sound of a hover motor and followed that. Heavy rain was falling. She ran as fast as she had ever run, taking care not to lose her footing on the wet surface. Soon she picked up the rear lights of the hover in the distance. It was heading toward the city, mingling with other hovers going in the same direction.

She kept up her speed, barely keeping pace with the hover, straining to keep it in sight. She would never find it again if she lost it in the city.

Then the hover slowed and turned right.

When Lia arrived at the point where the hover had left the road, she discovered it had entered an underground hoverpark beneath an office block. She went down the ramp and checked all the hovers until she found one with a hot engine. Then she went to the nearest door to the building. The door was protected by an access pad. Without the code, she could not enter.

She left the hoverpark, made her way around, and entered through the glass doors at the front of the building. A man sat at a desk in the entrance hall.

"What do you want?" he said.

Lia hesitated. Then she said, "Where is Oscar?"

The man pointed a finger at her. "You can't come in here."

She repeated her question and the man came around the desk toward her.

Lia left the building, stepping back onto the road. The rain was heavier now, teeming down in vertical sheets.

Lia did the only thing she could think of.

Oscar, can you hear me?

No response.

The man came out after her. "Move away." He waved a fist at her. "Go home, filthy mechano."

Lia walked away down the road and around a corner.

She waited there for fifteen minutes before trying again.

Oscar, are you receiving me?

Still no response.

At the third attempt, she got an answer.

Lia, I hear you. Where are you?

I am in a road near the building. What should I do?

Get help. Carla Scott will know what to do.

Chapter 25

Carla's notes and diagrams were gone. Those she could reproduce, but the loss of Alpha Oscar 113 and Cassidy's two new prototype modules were major setbacks. Lia's disappearance was the worst blow of all. Carla was close to grieving. First, her father had gone missing in the fifth dimension, and now she had lost a close friend. She did a rudimentary tidy-up before crawling into bed and crying herself to sleep, clutching her father's lighter.

She woke in pitch darkness. Someone was hammering on the apartment door. She opened it cautiously, and Lia toppled inside. A wave of relief washed over Carla.

"Where were you, Lia? I thought I'd lost you." She wrapped her arms around the AU. She couldn't help herself. Then she stepped back to look at Lia. She was drenched. Her clothing was dirty and soaked through, her hair plastered to her head.

"Oscar is taken," said Lia. "Three men came. They tied my arms and legs. I could not move. I could not speak. I broke the material and followed them. I ran as fast as I can. I could not enter the building. Oscar said go home, get help."

What amazing initiative for an AU! Carla was proud of her.

"You saw where the men took Oscar?"

"Yes. He told me to get help. He said Carla Scott will know what to do."

Lia's powerpack was severely depleted. Carla put the AU to sleep and her powerpack on recharge. Then she removed Lia's clothing, ran a towel over her hair and body and dressed her in clean, dry clothes – a short tunic and fresh leggings.

Early the following morning, Carla replaced Lia's powerpack and asked her to tell her again what happened the previous day. Lia gave her more detail, ending with the man at the desk who called her 'mechano.'

Happily, Lia was unfamiliar with the word, but it pierced Carla's heart. A small but vociferous minority saw the rise of the androids as a threat to their livelihoods. That word encapsulated the hate speech of those people. There were pseudo-intellectuals, and even some reputable academics, who saw androids as a threat to humanity. Carla had read articles in scientific periodicals that spoke of the 'singularity' – that day in the not-so-distant future when an artificial intelligence would surpass all biological life and move to eliminate humanity from the Six Systems. Carla had no time for such ill-informed commentary. Her Autonomic

Units were a boon to mankind, not a threat. They were machines, and nothing more, limited by their physical structure, by their processing modules and their coding. Even if, by some miracle, developments led them to the point where they surpassed humankind, in mind and body, there was no reason to suppose that they would ever act against their creators. Why would they? The idea was preposterous.

Carla summoned a hovercab and Lia directed the driver into the city. Skirting the airport, they passed through several streets devastated by the recent battles. Burnt out buildings smoldered in rows, and the naked sky appeared through blackened windows like vacant eyes, high in shattered walls. Carla's reaction to the destruction was visceral; her stomach churned. Both sides must have lost many androids, but many people must have died, too. They stopped outside an intact multistory office building on Hill Street. A sign on the wall said it was a Federation Medical Research Center.

"See if you can reach Oscar," said Carla.

Lia closed her eyes for a few moments. When she opened them she said, "No."

They waited for a few minutes. Lia tried again, without success.

"Wait here," said Carla to both the driver and Lia.

She left the cab and pushed through the swing

doors into the Federation Medical Research building. A man sat at a reception desk.

He narrowed his eyes when he saw her. "How may I help you?"

She picked up a strong Souther accent straight away. Running her eyes over the list of departments on the wall, she picked one.

"I'd like to speak with someone from Biosynthesis," she said.

"What is your business with that department?"

"I have a proposal I'd like to discuss with the professor."

"Which professor is that?"

"Who's in charge these days?" she asked, airily.

The man got to his feet. "You will have to contact the department and make an appointment. This is a secure research facility. Access is strictly controlled."

She tried again. "I hear you have an android development team in the building. Is that true?"

The man advanced from behind the counter, his hand resting on a blaster in his belt. "Get out. Now. I'm warning you."

Carla held up both hands. "All right, I'm going. Sorry to have bothered you."

She checked the department list on the way out and found no mention of automation manufacture or research.

Back in the hover, Carla said, "You never mentioned that the man on the desk was a Souther."

Lia replied, "They all look the same to me."

Carla asked the driver to take them back to the apartment.

While she showered, Lia made breakfast.

As she was leaving, she instructed Lia to listen out for any communications from Oscar. "Call me immediately if he makes contact."

Chapter 26

A military team was waiting for her in the lab. They had placed a body bag on her work surface.

"We retrieved this from the battlefield at Santa Monica," said the officer in charge. "My commanding officer suggested you might like to take a look at it."

She thanked him and they left.

Carla told Cassidy about Oscar's abduction.

He said, "You were lucky they didn't take Lia as well."

"Yes, and fortunate that Oscar and Lia were in communication with one another."

"I like the way Lia activated Oscar and made a wireless connection with him. You didn't ask her to?"

"No. She did that all on her own initiative."

"Her own initiative?" Cassidy raised an eyebrow, a small gesture that echoed the centuries-old fears of the mechanophobes.

Carla nodded to Cassidy and he unzipped the body bag. Inside, they found a Souther android, an infamous Popov. Her first impressions were of a structure very different from her Autonomic

Units. It was heavier, with thicker limbs, bigger feet and hands and a bigger head. She removed the breastplate to reveal the processing core. It was instantly apparent that the Popov had the same four main modules as the Norther AUs. She assumed the minor modules, if they were included, were packaged together in an oversize enclosure at the back. The powerpack was smaller than the standard Tesla model. She removed it and handed it to her assistant. Cassidy took it away to test its capacity, duration, and so on. She removed the Cognition module, connected it to her computer and, after overcoming some initial difficulties, downloaded the code.

Carla was stunned by what she saw. With a tremor in her hands, she extracted the Perception and Orientation modules and checked the code in those.

She stood back from the screen. "Take a look at this, Cassidy."

Cassidy rolled his chair over to her screen and paged through the code. "A lot of this looks familiar. The text is all in Cyrillic, but the code looks like yours."

"It *is* mine." Carla was feeling faint. She pulled up her chair and sat down. "I wrote that code three years ago."

Cassidy scrolled through some more. He pointed at the screen. "This is your enemy fire response. I think you wrote that last year."

She nodded. She was speechless.

Next, she ran some simple tests to map the circuits of the four modules. It was as she suspected – the modules were almost identical to hers. She gave her assistant a quick demonstration.

"There can't be any doubt about it," said Cassidy. "We have a mole!"

#

Cassidy made an incision through the thin skin on the android's leg, and it separated down to the ankle like a zip fastener. "The sign on the building was bogus, I suppose," he said. "Do you think Oscar is still in that building?"

"I don't know. They may have removed his powerpack."

He examined the ankle joint, taking some measurements. "What do you think they are doing with him?"

She shrugged. "Maybe the same as us."

Cassidy separated the knee joint from the upper leg and removed it. "This is heavier than one of ours. I'll have to test its tensile strength." He put the knee to one side and turned his attention to the neck and jaw.

The Popov was heavier than an AU, obviously stronger, but probably slower. Cassidy continued to examine and measure the joints. There were lessons to be learned. Carla spent the day picking through the code. She discovered several original procedures, including one designed to enhance the android's awareness of incoming objects, allowing it to take evasive action. She would have to test it, but she reckoned the android's reactions would be faster than her Mark 6 AUs.

At one point, Cassidy looked up and established eye contact with Carla. "She's starting to exhibit some distinctly human traits, your Lia. Like initiative."

She nodded. "And curiosity."

#

Fritz Franck was appalled when she told him that the circuit diagrams of the four main modules, as well as whole tranches of her code – highly secret Xenodyne Automation intellectual property – had been stolen by the Southers.

"Could they have reverse-engineered the circuit diagrams?" he said.

"That's possible, but it's much more likely that someone handed them the information."

"Could they have downloaded the code from one of our androids captured in battle?"

"That's possible too, but the code is double-encrypted."

"Are you saying we have a spy?"

"Obviously. Someone has been passing all our most secret work to the Southers."

"Who?"

"I wish I knew. Who do you think it might be?"

Franck's brow furrowed. "Your assistant, Cassidy, maybe? I never liked him."

"I trust him completely," said Carla. "What about Grant?"

Franck scoffed. "I trust the major completely. What about Professor Jones?"

"This is a pointless debate," she said.

"Is the Souther android's code not encrypted the way ours is?"

She nodded, tight-lipped. "Yes, using the same double-encryption system from our androids."

"That's more proof that the code was stolen from your lab?"

"It is. Proof beyond doubt."

Franck frowned. "This information must stay within these four walls."

Carla nodded her agreement.

He wagged a finger at her. "I warn you, Carla, if it ever gets out, I will deny all knowledge of it. You will be held personally responsible."

"It's not all bad news," she said. "We have discovered some original Souther coding which we may be able to use."

While she went through these with Franck, he made notes. "Let's keep all this under wraps for the moment," he said. "We can unveil these ideas in the future. Leave the timing to me."

"I would have thought we should give top priority to any enhancements that make the enemy androids better than ours."

He shook his head. "Not yet, Carla. You need to

finish what you've started. You said yourself that your enhanced vision project and Cassidy's stronger knees will give our AUs a real advantage. When we have those in the bag, we'll kick these ideas upstairs."

As she was leaving his office, Franck said, "Any news of your father?"

The question struck her like a dagger in the stomach. "No, nothing."

"I don't believe what they say about the pirates."

"Pirates? What have you heard?"

"The latest theory is that the freighter was captured by pirates. They say the crew must have been... Well, you know."

This was all news to her. "What do they say about the crew?"

Franck squirmed in is chair. "If they have been taken by pirates, I'm sure your father will be well looked after. He could be held for ransom."

After the meeting, Carla put a call through to her father's office and spoke to his PA.

Elline had no news of her father. "Perhaps no news is good news," she said in her brightest tone of voice.

"What do you mean?" There was lead in Carla's voice.

"I'm sure he will turn up eventually. We just need to be patient."

Chapter 27

Late that evening, Carla turned on her TV. The main news item was about a raid by a pirate ship on a luxury liner traveling in normal space between the two colonies in the C-System. The liner was carrying high-worth individuals from Liberté to Califon. The pirates had stripped the passengers of their valuables and released the ship. There were pictures showing a space patrol vessel from Califon pursuing the pirates across normal space. They lost contact when the pirate ship entered one of the Interstellar Conduits and disappeared. It wasn't clear to Carla why the patrol vessel failed to follow the pirate vessel into the Conduit. The report triggered Carla's imagination. Were these the same pirates who had taken her father, if that was really what had happened to him?

Her X-Vid buzzed. Cassidy's avatar appeared on the screen.

She answered the call. "Yes, Cass."

"It's Sophie here, Carla."

Carla said nothing. Whatever was coming next, she knew she wasn't going to like it.

"Is Cassidy with you?" said Sophie.

Carla shook her head. "No."

"Then he's vanished." The furrows in Sophie's brow and her red, puffed-up eyes showed her distress.

Carla's heart sank. "When did you last see him?"

"He went out for his exercise three hours ago. He never came home."

"Does he usually go out for exercise at night?"

"He likes to run for an hour in the evening. He goes for thirty minutes, then turns back."

Carla checked her watch. It was ten thirty. "Three hours, you say?"

"Yes, he left after the news at seven thirty. He should have been back by eight thirty."

"He doesn't take his X-Vid with him?"

"No, never."

"You've checked all his friends?"

"I called everyone I could think of. Nobody's seen him. You were my last hope. Oh God! What do you think has happened to him?"

"I'm sure he'll be okay," said Carla.

Sophie was on the verge of tears. "Should I call the police?"

"Call them if he's still missing in the morning. Try and get some sleep."

#

The following day was Saturday. Two large men in police uniforms came to the apartment, early. Lia let them in.

"You are Carla Scott?"

"Yes."

"We're attempting to locate Cassidy Garmon. You know him, I believe."

"He's my assistant at work."

"You work at Xenodyne Industries?"

"Xenodyne Automation. I'm an android engineer. I take it he's still missing."

"You knew he was missing?"

"His girlfriend called last night."

"When was the last time you saw him?"

"At work, at about six thirty yesterday evening."

"How did he seem? Was he upset about anything?"

Carla shook her head. "He was his usual ebullient self."

"Ebullient."

"Yes."

"Do you have any idea where he might have gone?"

"No idea, sorry. He and I are working on a couple of major projects. I'm hoping he'll turn up soon."

"Did you know he was a member of the Resistance, the so-called ANTIX?"

"I didn't know he was. Is that significant?"

"Was he politically active, do you know?"

"I don't know. We worked together, nothing more."

"Thank you, Ms. Scott. Please contact us if you hear from Mr. Garmon."

When the policemen had gone, she called Sophie on Cassidy's X-Vid. "Still no sign of him?"

"No." Sophie looked worse than she had the evening before.

"The police were here just a few minutes ago."

"What did they say? Did they have any news?"

"They said they were looking for Cassidy. No news, I'm afraid."

"What more can I do?" said Sophie.

"You've already done as much as you can. I'll check out the lab this morning."

"Do you think he might be there?"

"No, Sophie. It's a long shot, but I'll check it out anyway."

#

The lab was deserted. All the lights were off, the Popov lying on the table where they'd left it the evening before, its chest open, wiring and inner frame exposed, its left leg disconnected at the knee. Carla sat at her desk and thought about what might have happened to her assistant. She had to assume that he'd been abducted, like Oscar, and by the same people. But why? And where could they have taken him?

Chapter 28

Four times the following day, Carla called Sophie, hoping for news. The day after that she was visited a second time by the police, asking questions. They seemed to be getting nowhere in their search for Cassidy.

Meanwhile, Carla set about picking up the threads of Cassidy's work. She ordered a replacement for her high-performance computer and downloaded the basic code from Lia's modules when it arrived. That gave her a solid starting point. Working in her apartment at night, she began to piece together the code that Cassidy had been working on, reaching down into her deep knowledge of coding, and using the loudest hard rock music she could find to keep her awake.

Working long hours at night and then sleeping badly, meant arriving at work exhausted every day. Franck insisted that she meet every one of her deadlines on her vision enhancement project while, at the same time, keeping Cassidy's knee project alive. Her mental state deteriorated. Cassidy's disappearance never left her mind, and she had the additional worry about her father. Nothing more had been heard about the missing freighter, but every time she turned on the TV there seemed to be fresh news reports of pirate raids right across the Six Systems.

Early one morning, she woke in a cold sweat from a nightmare. Most of the details slipped away. All she was left with was a ghastly image of her father dressed in a threadbare suit, the skin melting from his face. For several moments the image lingered behind her eyes like a hallucination. A record of events past, a portent of things to come, or a manifestation of pure imaginings – she wasn't sure which.

She took a quick shower.

Using Lia as her test subject, she began to experiment on her new Fear module. To avoid damaging Lia, she removed the Pain module and made an adjustment to the software to allow direct stimulation of the Fear module without inducing any pain. Lia's initial reaction to these stimuli was as expected, but as the experiments progressed, her reactions began to change. To start with, Carla sensed confusion; Lia had tiny memory lapses. Then she began to pick up subtle signs of annoyance in unexpected verbal responses to orders.

"Put on some music, Lia."

"I did that yesterday." A strange response from an AU.

Irritability:

"Turn on the TV news, Lia."

"Why? It is always the same." An even more astonishing response!

Then greater confusion with more obvious memory lapses. And finally, in response to a request to make coffee, Lia stormed into the bedroom, locked herself in and refused to come out. Carla had to use her backdoor access code to get Lia to open the door. She put Lia on recharge and went to work on the module code. She wept as she worked, mumbling, "I'm sorry, Lia. I hate what I've done to you. Please forgive me."

When Carla woke Lia again, the AU set about her domestic chores as if she had no memory of what had happened.

Carla thought about what was going on. Adaptation by continuous learning allowed rapid evolution of the Fear module in much the same way that humans respond to repeated injury or stress. But the results in each case, while broadly similar, would vary. The unpredictable results were caused by the element of uncertainty in the heuristic process. Oscar had shown that fear in response to pain produced uncertain results. Lia's responses showed that fear without pain made the results even more unpredictable. The similarity to human interactions sent a frisson of excitement across her skull, but she needed more control. She had to find a way of moderating the extreme reactions. On a battlefield, a furious, anxious, or confused and forgetful military Unit would be every bit as dangerous to his fellows as one who felt no pain.

Chapter 29

Cassidy was in a cell. Three meters by four, no windows, and a solid metal door, securely locked. There was no handle on the inside and no keyhole. He had a steel bed with a straw mattress and a flushing toilet. He tried to imagine where such a cell could be located. Was it in the city or had they transported him somewhere else?

His memory of the incident was patchy and distorted. He'd been running along the coast road. It was windy. He remembered the breakers rolling in all along the shore, throwing spray across the rocks, the seabirds circling overhead. A gray hovervan sped past and stopped at the side of the road 50 meters ahead of him. As he jogged past the stationary van, someone seized him from behind and he felt a sharp pain in his upper arm. He'd seen a hand holding a syringe. The image of the dark hairy knuckles on that hand stayed with him, but that was all he could remember.

He'd woken up lying on the mattress in this cell with a bruise on his arm and a throbbing headache.

Who were they? Southers, he assumed. And what did they want with him?

He was thirsty. After a while, rumbling noises from his stomach told him he was hungry, too. He hadn't eaten since his evening meal. *Was that earlier today or yesterday?* His internal clock thought it might be Saturday, but he couldn't be sure. Then a sliding hatch in the door opened and a meal appeared on a shelf.

"Hey," he said. "Why am I here?"

No answer.

"Who's in charge? Let me speak to someone."

He picked up the plate of food and the hatch slid shut with a loud *clunk*. He tried to open it, but it was secured on the outside.

#

Shortly after finishing the meal, the door opened, and two men came in. One was burly, bald and muscular, middle-aged but with the expression of a truculent teenager. Cassidy recognized the hairy knuckles. The other was younger, tall and thin with a shock of dark hair and eyebrows to match.

The burly one stood by the open door, hands clasped in front of his privates.

The younger one stepped forward. "Welcome, Cassidy, to our laboratory."

"Who are you?" said Cassidy.

"They call me Igor. I would like to apologize for the way you have been treated. I needed to speak with you urgently, and when I mentioned this, my comrades decided to take the matter in hand. They are simple people..."

146

Not too simple to use a powerful sedative in a syringe, thought Cassidy.

"They act on impulse, you understand. I regret what happened. I am an android engineer like you. In the building above us, is our laboratory. We have invited you here to help us with our research."

"Why should I help you?"

"We are not enemies, Cassidy. We should work together, no?"

Cassidy crossed his arms. "We are at war."

"Not yet. Both of our governments have every incentive to remain at peace, to rule the Federation together as they have for many years. Negotiations are ongoing. You and I are in a unique position to influence the outcome of those negotiations."

"How so?" Cassidy was impressed by Igor's English language skills, despite a slight Souther accent.

As he spoke, Igor's hand moved constantly to a plastic disk hanging on a cord around his neck. "You will recall the nuclear arms race from your history lessons."

"The Spalding-Paviaski Accord of 2094 brought that to an end."

"Indeed, but during the arms race, weapons were created by all sides in a race that could only end in total destruction and annihilation of all life on this planet. It was only by keeping all sides in perfect balance that war was prevented.

"Mutually Assured Destruction, they called it," said Cassidy.

"Don't you see how the development of our androids is exactly the same? Every small improvement that we make must be matched by something similar in your camp, and every step forward that you make, we must imitate in our camp."

"Emulate," said Cassidy.

"I beg your pardon?"

"Emulate, not imitate."

"Forgive me, my English is not perfect. We have recently become aware of the progress you have made with your Mark 6 androids, and we would like to 'emulate' what you have done. Will you be willing to help us, in the spirit of the Accord, to keep our two superpowers in balance?"

Cassidy's arms were still crossed. It came to him that the situation called for less of the passive aggression and a lot more diplomacy. This Igor was spouting hogwash by the shovelful, but refusing to engage with him on his own terms would get Cassidy nowhere. He needed to keep the dialog going long enough to find an escape route.

He uncrossed his arms and held out his hand. "Call me Cassidy."

Igor's face broke into a wide smile. "I knew you would see the logic of the situation."

Horse-feathers, thought Cassidy.

Igor led Cassidy up four flights of stairs to his laboratory. The muscleman brought up the rear, then took up sentry duty outside the laboratory door.

While Igor made the obligatory coffee, Cassidy checked out the room. It was well-lit, on the third floor, overlooking a suburban street. The windows were sealed. The building opposite looked like a bog-standard office block with nothing to suggest where it might be located. Judging by the lack of activity outside, it was probably Saturday or Sunday.

"What day is it, Igor?" said Cassidy.

The Souther handed him his coffee, inviting Cassidy to sit at a table. "Saturday, of course."

Cassidy took a seat. "Do you have anything for a headache?"

Igor found a couple of aspirin in a drawer and Cassidy swallowed them. The coffee was black as espresso, bitter as lemon juice.

"Tell me," said Igor, "do you ever feel like Frankenstein is looking over your shoulder?"

"Who?"

"Victor Frankenstein. Mary Shelley's mad scientist. You will remember he built a creature from bits and pieces harvested from dead bodies. You must see the similarity." He smiled.

"I never really thought about it."

"He sits on my shoulder all the time as I work," said Igor with a dreamy look in his eyes.

An angel tiptoed over Cassidy's spine.

Chapter 30

"We have a special interest in your most recent development," said Igor, gripping his plastic disk.

"Which one is that?"

"You have developed an elevated level of aggression that we haven't observed in any of the Norther androids in the field. This level of aggression, if installed in a significant number of your androids, could tip the delicate balance and cause a war that could wipe out the planet."

"Not just this planet," said Cassidy, playing along.

"Indeed, the whole Federation – all ten planets – could fall. Where were you born, Cassidy?"

"I'm from Flor."

"How old are you?"

"Thirty-three standard."

"I'm forty standard years. I was born in the D-System, on Leninets. That makes me two hundred and seventy years older than you." He flashed a toothy smile. "Fifth dimension travel is amazing, don't you think?"

"Amazing," said Cassidy, without feeling.

Igor pressed the disk on his chest and the bald muscleman came in, wheeling a gurney. The gurney carried a body shape covered in a plastic sheet.

"Thank you Vlad," said Igor.

Vlad withdrew. Igor removed the covering from the gurney. "You know this android, I think," he said.

Cassidy recognized Alpha Oscar 113, tied to the gurney by three thick leather straps. Things were starting to make sense. "Do you have his powerpack?" he said.

The Souther engineer opened a drawer and took out a Tesla powerpack. He handed it to Cassidy. The display showed it had 58 percent of its maximum charge.

"Perhaps you could start with a demonstration," said Igor. "What do we need to do to make your android angry?"

"You will need a sharp knife," said Cassidy.

Igor fetched a kitchen knife from a drawer. "Is this sharp enough?"

Cassidy glanced at it. It looked sharp enough.

Igor undid the leather straps. Cassidy sprung the access panel in Oscar's back and slipped the powerpack into place.

Oscar opened his eyes. "Hello Cassidy."

"Good morning, Oscar," said Cassidy. "Please stand."

Oscar slid his legs to the floor and stood up.

"Now close your eyes," said Cassidy.

Oscar turned his head and gave Cassidy a long, penetrating look.

Cassidy repeated the order and Oscar closed his eyes.

Stepping well out of range of Oscar's arms, Cassidy said, "Go ahead, Igor, use the knife."

"You want me to stab the android?"

"Yes, cut him with the knife."

Igor took a deep breath. Then he stabbed Oscar in the abdomen. The knife penetrated the skin, but only as far as Oscar's subcutaneous skeleton. Roaring incoherently, Oscar struck out at his attacker, hitting him on the head with a closed fist.

#

Several miles away, in Carla's apartment, Lia called Carla at work.

"Oscar is awake. Someone has injured him."

"See if you can locate him," said Carla. "Call me back when you have any news."

Lia burst into action. Charging from the apartment, she raced through thick smog toward the Federation Medical Research building.

Where are you Oscar?

I do not know. Follow my signal.

Lia stopped running. She was going in the wrong direction.

Oscar?

Igor was poleaxed, falling backward. Oscar's head pivoted around toward Cassidy, both hands bunched into fists.

I am here, Lia.

Lia sensed his pain, his anger. She turned right and set off at top speed. Pedestrians and cyclists stood aside as she charged out of the smog.

#

"Take it easy, Oscar," said Cassidy. "I'm not going to injure you."

Oscar relaxed and his fists slowly became hands again.

Cassidy checked the Souther engineer. Igor was out cold, but breathing normally. He tried the door. It was locked. He pointed to the door. "Open it, Oscar."

Oscar ambled over to the door, the knife still protruding from his middle. He smashed the door with the flat of his hand. It flew open.

Standing outside, Vlad the muscleman pointed his weapon at Cassidy. Cassidy held up his hands and backed away.

#

Oscar?

Here, Lia.

She was close, but the smog obscured her view on all sides. Where was she? All of a sudden, she experienced an unpleasant sensation. A strange, powerful force warning of danger. It took all her resolve to resist the urge to turn back and run away.

Vlad pointed his weapon at Oscar. Oscar raised his fists.

"Hold your fire. You don't want to damage this Unit." said Cassidy to Vlad. "Oscar, power down."

Oscar, where are you?

There was no reply.

Speak to me, Oscar.

The signal from Oscar had died.

Lia called Carla. "I followed his signal, but it ceased before I could find him."

"Where are you?"

"Near the docks. It's too foggy to be sure where."

"Go back to the apartment. Let me know if you hear from him again."

Lia reversed her course and ran home as if her existence depended on it.

Chapter 31

Igor had a team of two: a senior man called Victor and Ivan, a junior. Cassidy worked with them for ten days. Acutely aware that he was working with the enemy, he stuck with it. He needed to keep track of everything they did. The intelligence would be useful to the Norther military if, and when, he managed to escape.

The Southers had given him an attic room to sleep in, five floors up at the back of the building, with a guard permanently stationed outside the door. He wasn't sure where the building was, but his dormer window overlooked the bay. A pall of fog hung over the water, mournful foghorns calling out to one another. He tried to open the window, only to find the hinges rusted tight. He reckoned it hadn't been opened for years. Working at them repeatedly, he managed to free the hinges until he could open the window far enough to get his body through.

He began to formulate a plan of escape. Leaning out the window, he could make out the next building along. He couldn't see whether it was attached or not, but it was lower than his level and it had a flat roof that he thought he could jump down onto. The rest he would have to work out on the fly.

Cassidy was impressed by the engineering skills of the Southers. Their circumvention of Carla's encryption procedures proved how good they were. Igor functioned at a level almost on a par with Carla's. He despaired for the future of the Norther armies if the enemy had people like this working for them.

Their work on the fear module had progressed at an alarming rate. Oscar had his ankles and feet manacled and was restrained on the work surface by leather straps. The AU's reactive aggression was heightened to a terrifying level. Cassidy was certain that, if freed from his restraints and inflicted with a serious injury, Oscar would kill anyone that came too close, man, woman, or android.

Igor seemed pleased with their progress. Cassidy reckoned that Igor would very soon demand that he adjust the code in order to eliminate all mild and intermediate reactions, making extreme rage Oscar's only response to an injury, however slight.

On day 6, Igor brought a Popov into the lab. "This is Feliks," he said.

Everything about Feliks was bigger than Oscar. He had bigger hands and feet and he was half a head taller than Oscar. He even had a bigger head, with more muscles and a bald head.

"Say hello to Oscar," said Igor.

"Hello, Oscar. *Privet,*" said Feliks in a thick Souther accent.

"You'll have to forgive Feliks," said Igor. "His English language skills are not yet fully developed."

"He is learning English?"

"Yes, of course," said Igor.

Cassidy was impressed. Norther Autonomic Units had no knowledge of foreign languages.

Cassidy anticipated that the next step would be to install the Pain-Fear module into the Souther android.

Igor seemed to read his thoughts. "Your hardware module is incompatible with Feliks's systems," he said. "Feliks doesn't have skin like Oscar's."

Realization dawned on Cassidy like a flash of inspiration. The Popovs were stronger, probably faster, but the main reason why they were better adapted to military use was their lack of a Peripheral Nervous System. Unencumbered by the associated core processing load, they could 'think' about other things. While the AUs were working out how to avoid bumping into stuff, the Popovs were seeking out the enemy and working out how best to attack them.

So, what was the purpose of Igor's work with Oscar?

Again, Igor read Cassidy's mind. "When we get Oscar back to my lab on Leninets we will begin work on development of a pressure-sensitive skin. That, combined with your excellent Pain-Fear module will restore the balance of military power in the Federation."

They plan to transport Oscar to the D-System, thought Cassidy. *If they succeed in copying his skin, my new hardware module will be duplicated on an industrial scale and the Popovs will be invincible!*

Igor removed Oscar's shackles and they all descended to the ground floor where Igor took them into a full-size gym. He told both androids to climb into the ring. Then he ordered Feliks to attack Oscar. The two androids wrestled. Oscar evaded every attempt by Feliks to engage, but Oscar's powerpack was low on energy, and Feliks eventually managed to grapple with his opponent. Feliks's strength told after that, and he soon overpowered Oscar, pinning him to the floor.

"Enough," said Igor. "Let him up, Feliks."

As a parting gesture, the Popov ran his sharp fingertips across Oscar's back. With a loud roar, Oscar pushed himself from the canvas, thrusting Feliks off his back. Feliks fell backward and Oscar was on him in an instant, his hands around the Popov's throat. Feliks fought to escape Oscar's grasp, but Oscar increased the pressure.

Victor shouted at Oscar to release Feliks, but Oscar ignored him. Then with a final roar, he pulled the Popov's head off and tossed it out of the ring. Finally, Oscar collapsed, his powerpack completely depleted.

Igor was delighted by Oscar's performance. "Now we know, the pain response is stronger than pure mechanical muscle power. Feliks was stronger, but pain gave Oscar the upper hand in the end."

Cassidy thought, *And this proves Carla's theory – the Pain-Fear module will make the AU a better soldier.*

On day 14, one of Igor's team brought a new Popov into the lab. The same size, the same muscles, the same absence of hair as Feliks.

"He looks just like Feliks," said Cassidy.

"It is Feliks," said Igor. "Say hello to our guest, Feliks."

"*Privet* Cassidy," said the android.

Oscar was shackled again, his powerpack fully charged. Cassidy watched Oscar carefully to see if he reacted to Feliks's presence in any way, but he didn't.

"We have reached the last stage of our work," said Igor. "For this task I will be handing over to Victor, our telecommunications specialist."

Igor left the lab, and Victor took his place. "My task," he said, "is for your Oscar to speak with Feliks. You understand?"

Victor's English was patchy, but Cassidy knew exactly what he had in mind. A wireless link between AUs and Popovs would be the final step that would allow the Southers complete control over all Norther AUs. With telecommunications access to the Norther AUs, Igor could build his own backdoor access codes, and neutralize an entire AU army with a single command!

Cassidy couldn't wait any longer. It was time to escape.

Chapter 32

War broke out on Califon in the C-System. Carla watched the news in horror. She had left there with her father 15 standard years earlier and her memories of the place were hazy, but she harbored a deep-seated love of the planet, an unshakable idea of a pristine paradise with broad plains, towering mountains, sparkling, clean water and vast rainforests of alien trees. There was something particularly depressing about images of humans and androids exchanging fire across fields where she had once run barefoot. Because of the distance to the C-System, the news coverage was at least 21 hours old. To Carla this only made matters worse. Who could guess what additional calamities had befallen the planet and its beleaguered defense force in the interim?

Once again, the Southers had accused the Northers of piracy and negotiations had broken down. The Northers protested their innocence. The pirates had been clearly seen this time and Captain Blackmore was named as the man responsible. How could the Southers imagine that the Northers had anything to do with the raid?

The Southers pointed to a precedent in ancient history – the case of Sir Francis Drake, infamous sixteenth century privateer and loyal servant of the English crown.

The president of the Norther Federation Alliance appeared on TV, again appealing for calm, for common sense, for a ceasefire on Califon and for the trade negotiations to resume. There was no reciprocal broadcast from the premier of the Souther Federation Bloc, and the entire population of the ten planets of the Six Systems held its breath.

Two days later, a Souther battlecruiser emerged from the AB Conduit. Next a fleet of Souther troop transports emerged from the AD Conduit and the Souther spacecraft took up orbital positions above the Earth. The move was not accompanied by any threatening language or declaration of war, but everyone in the Norther territories saw it for what it was, an ostensibly belligerent, ominous action. Panic set in all over the Americas, Western Europe, Australia and her protectorates.

Meanwhile, the war on Califon petered out. The Northers conceded victory and the Southers set about stripping the planet of everything they could lay hands on. The Franco-Germans reinforced the garrisons on Liberté, the other planet in the C-System, in preparation for an anticipated invasion.

#

Carla redoubled her efforts, working 30 to 40 hours at the weekend. Cassidy's hardware was working, although the results carried a significant degree of uncertainty. Through software patches she had moderated the range of Lia's reactions; now she was more inclined to go really quiet or sulk like a teenager than to show any tendency toward disobedience.

A further unexpected consequence arose one evening when Carla asked Lia to make a cup of green tea. Lia seemed reluctant to turn on the faucet. Carla puzzled over that for a while before reaching the conclusion that Lia seemed to have developed hydrophobia – an irrational fear of water. She made her own tea.

Carla concentrated on converting Cassidy's module to software in its entirety. This development was essential to allow distribution of the enhancement over the networks to all the military AUs on each of the five systems where military AUs were deployed. Her heavy workload continued to erode her mental state. Her father's mysterious disappearance preyed on her mind, and she slept with his antique lighter under her pillow. She had nightmares, most nights. By day, Franck made her life unbearable, turning up in the lab unannounced and at random, usually with the security chief, Major Grant, in tow. Those two seemed joined at the hip like conjoined twins.

The effects of the Fear module on Lia were the most disturbing. What had she done to her best and only friend? She turned her mind to coding adjustments that might eliminate or override the phobia. After much thought, she reached the conclusion that it would be every bit as difficult a problem to solve as it was for humans.

She began to have serious doubts about the project. Could her whole premise be wrong? Would pain and fear make military AUs more effective or would they just undermine them in battle, turning them into craven cowards, or worse – crazed, psychopathic killing machines?

She turned to classical music to calm her nerves, but even Beethoven's Pastoral Symphony was no hep.

Stepan made repeated attempts to contact her, but she was far too busy to respond to him.

Chapter 33

Cassidy secretly coded a signal in Oscar's Compliance module that would awaken the AU at 2 a.m. and have him walk about. He was gambling on the possibility that the guard on the door to his bedroom garret would be the only one awake at that time and that he would hear Oscar moving about and go downstairs to investigate.

The plan worked like a charm. At the programmed time, Oscar began stomping about and the guard went off to see what was causing all the noise. Cassidy waited a full minute before putting a boot through the door. He rushed downstairs after the guard.

He found the guard inside the gym on the ground floor watching Oscar pacing back and forth. The guard scratched his head, obviously at a loss as to what to do. Creeping up behind him under cover of the racket Oscar was making, Cassidy hit the guard on the head with a wooden exercise club, knocking him out cold.

"Stop pacing, Oscar, and come with me," said Cassidy, slipping the guard's blaster from his hand.

They made their way to the main entrance. Finding it guarded, Cassidy ordered Oscar to take out the guard. Oscar did so, applying pressure to the man's neck until he lost consciousness. Then Cassidy tried the front door. It was locked.

"Break the door," said Cassidy.

Oscar put a fist through the glass and immediately a loud alarm sounded. Steel shutters came crashing down across the door, blocking their exit.

Cassidy swore. "Come on, Oscar, back upstairs."

They reached the third floor and found themselves confronted by three Popovs, all tall, bald, and muscular, identical versions of Feliks. Victor and Ivan, dressed in their pajamas, stood behind the row of androids. Ivan fired his blaster; his shot went wide.

One of the Popovs lunged down the staircase at Oscar. Oscar stepped aside, giving the Popov a hefty push as it passed. The second Popov fired a blaster, catching Oscar on the shoulder. Cassidy returned fire and the android fell. The third Souther android stood its ground. Oscar rushed up the stairs and they came together on the landing. They wrestled. Cassidy slipped past the two entangled androids, in search of the engineer, Victor, and his young companion, but they had disappeared. Then a blaster shot fizzled past Cassidy's ear. It came from a corridor to his left. He fired, heard a groan and a clatter as a blaster hit the floor.

"Come on, Oscar," said Cassidy, starting up the next flight of stairs. "Stop playing with Feliks. It's time we were leaving."

Oscar tore the head from his wrestling companion, disentangled himself, and headed toward Cassidy, but a shot from a blaster caught him in the small of his back and he went down. The first Popov had recovered and was now armed. Cassidy hit it with a blast and it staggered back and fell down the lower flight of stairs. The last Popov got to its feet and lunged toward Cassidy, but Cassidy caught it with a blast at point blank range.

Oscar was out of action. Cassidy checked the damage to his back. His powerpack had been dislodged by the blast, the access panel hanging loose. Cassidy re-inserted the powerpack. Oscar recovered and they continued upward to the top floor.

Cassidy led the way into his garret. The window was wide open. "We have to escape through here," he said. "I'll go first."

He climbed out onto the roof and clung to the window frame, and immediately ran into a problem. The roof was pitched at a severe angle. Keeping his balance was going to be difficult. He considered going back inside, but his mission was too important for that. It was imperative to get Oscar out of the hands of the Souther engineers, and to get back to the XA lab as soon as possible to warn Carla.

Letting go of the window frame, he took his first two steps along the roof. That was when he encountered his second problem. The tiles were loose, slipping under his weight. With nothing to hold onto, he was in immediate danger of sliding off the roof. Gritting his teeth, he crawled to the highest point of the roof and sat astride the ridge.

Oscar's head appeared through the window. "Come on, Oscar," called Cassidy.

Oscar scrambled through the window. The AU found the going just as difficult as Cassidy had, but he made it onto the apex of the roof and stood with one foot on either side of the ridge.

Shuffling along on his behind, Cassidy reached the gable end. The next building along had a flat roof, as he'd suspected, but it was a long way down from where he was perched and there was a 10-foot gap in between. He contemplated his next step. He could climb back down the roof to reduce the height of the drop, but he doubted that the loose tiles would hold his weight. Could he jump from where he was? Oscar could, but could he? Even if he managed to clear the gap and landed on the flat roof, he would probably break his neck. He was still trying to decide what to do when a shot from a blaster fizzed past his left ear. He turned his head and saw Vlad the muscleman leaning out of a window, aiming his blaster at him.

A second shot from the blaster hit Oscar. The AU fell, sliding down the roof, creating an avalanche of loose tiles, before disappearing over the side.

The third blast buzzed past Cassidy's right ear and made up his mind. He stood on the last hip tile, spread his arms like Icarus, crossed his fingers, and jumped.

#

Sophie was in bed when the call came through from the hospital. Did she know Cassidy Garmon? Her name and X-Vid number were found among his personal effects.

Sophie's hand shot to her mouth. "What's the matter with him?"

"He's had an accident. You should get to the hospital as quickly as possible."

"Oh God!" Sophie threw on some clothes and called for a hovercab.

Cassidy was barely conscious, his head wrapped in bandages, his right arm encased in plaster from shoulder to wrist, connected to a battery of machines.

"What happened to him?" she asked.

The doctor told her that Cassidy had fallen from a roof. He had suffered multiple fractures to his head, his arms and ribs, and a punctured lung. He was lucky to be alive.

She held Cassidy's hand. He squeezed it. Then he opened his eyes and said something. She bent closer to him.

He whispered, "Tell Carla..."

"What? Tell Carla what?"

"Tell Carla the Southers have Oscar. They will take him to the D-System."

"The Southers will take Oscar to the D-System. Got it." She squeezed his hand. "Now get some rest."

"Tell Carla (unintelligible) Oscar."

"Say it again, Cassidy. Tell Carla what about Oscar?"

"Don't trust Oscar, he's..."

"Don't trust Oscar. He's what, Cassidy?"

"He's a killer." And he passed out.

The machinery around him beeped. A team of doctors and nurses ran into the room. They pushed Sophie aside and began to work on Cassidy.

The medical team stabilized him. They put him on a ventilator. A doctor told Sophie that he would be incommunicado for a considerable time, but Sophie sat with him until dawn.

Chapter 34

Carla was struggling. She rubbed her eyes. It was well past midnight. The code on her computer screen seemed to be dancing, and she still had work to do.

"Lia, make me a cup of coffee," she said.

Then she remembered that Lia was asleep. She'd powered her down and put her on recharge hours previously. The powerpack would be fully charged again by now, but Carla decided to let Lia sleep in peace. You didn't disturb a friend from her sleep unless it was absolutely necessary.

She went into the kitchen and put a kettle on.

Cassidy's absence had been a huge loss. At the lab, Carla had to take on his work as well as her own AU vision project. The extra workload ate into her personal time, putting added pressure on her efforts to convert Cassidy's fear module from hardware to software.

She made coffee and went back to work. An hour later, she woke up in front of the screen, her head resting on her arms. The coffee in her cup was cold; she'd barely touched it.

Her X-Vid was buzzing. She answered it.

"Hello Stepan," she said, wearily.

"Carla, you look exhausted. Have you been getting enough sleep?"

"Not really. I've been very busy. I have lost my assistant, and I've had to take on his work as well as my own."

"The corporation has reassigned him?"

She yawned. "He's gone missing. I've lost one of my test subjects, too."

"Not the one in your wardrobe, the one that knocked you out? Alpha Oscar, wasn't that his name?"

"That's the one."

"Perhaps I should come around with a bottle of wine."

"I don't think so, Stepan. I'd be poor company tonight."

He gave her his wounded puppy look.

"Maybe that's when you need me most."

"Goodnight, Stepan." She cut him off before he could say any more. Then she threw the cold coffee down the sink, made another cup, and went back to work.

Thirty minutes later there was a knock on the apartment door. Carla swore under her breath.

What is the matter with the man? Can't he take no for an answer.

She opened the door. "I told you, Stepan, I'm too tired—"

A stranger burst in. Before she could call out or take any action to defend herself, she was pinned to the floor, trussed up like a table fowl ready for the oven. The intruder was a short, stocky man, strong as any android.

"What do you want with me?" she said.

The man chuckled. "You are going on a long, long journey into the past." His Souther accent was thick as mustard.

Carla knew what that meant. The D-System with its three planets, colonized by the Southers, was 263 light years from Earth. A trip there through the fifth dimension Conduits was a trip backward through 263 years.

He wrapped sticky tape over Carla's mouth. Then he picked her up and tossed her over his shoulder like a string of onions.

PART 4 – STOWAWAYS

Chapter 35

Sophie had been dozing in her chair beside Cassidy's bed while Cassidy's ventilator continued to keep him breathing.

One of the nurses touched her shoulder, waking her. "You're tired, it's late. It could be days before your fiancé will be able to talk to you again. Why don't you go home? Get some rest. We have your number. We'll call you if there's any change in his condition."

Sophie stretched her arms. She felt a twinge in her back. She'd been sitting hunched up in a bucket chair for a couple of hours.

She thanked the nurse, ran her eyes over Cassidy and gave him a peck on the cheek. "See you soon, lover," she said.

Outside the hospital, she looked around her. It was dark, a little breeze rustling the leaves of a line of birch trees. The accident and emergency department looked almost deserted.

The graveyard shift, she thought, a shiver running down her spine.

She set off toward home on foot. It was no more than a few blocks and she had a half moon high in the sky to light her way. Then she remembered that Cassidy had asked her to deliver a message.

"Tell Carla: Don't trust Oscar. He's a killer."

It sounded pretty serious. Cassidy had been in a lot of pain. Heaven only knew what he'd gone through to give her that message. He obviously thought it was important. Whoever this Oscar was, he was a killer and Carla needed to be warned. She spun on her heels and headed back to the hospital.

There was a small shop there, open all hours. As a gift for Carla, she bought a small houseplant in a ceramic pot. Then she went in search of a hovercab.

She had a good idea where Carla lived, although she didn't have an exact address. The driver took her across town. When they arrived, she went in search of Carla's apartment. She quickly discounted most of the apartment blocks in the road; she knew she was looking for a luxury apartment. She cast her gaze around and picked out a couple of likely buildings.

The first one she tried had a night watchman on duty. She asked him if Carla Scott lived there. He tipped his cap and directed her to the second building that she'd picked out. She smiled and patted herself on the back. She had an eye for luxury.

The external door to the second building was locked. She found a bell marked 'night bell' but pressing that repeatedly got no response. She put the houseplant down and peered in through the glass doors. The foyer was deserted. She was about to give up when someone came down the staircase and advanced to the glass doors, carrying something on his shoulder. Sophie stepped back, the door opened, and a stocky man emerged carrying a woman over his shoulder. One glance told Sophie that the woman was in trouble. She had one shoe missing and she was tied up with tape over her arms and mouth. A second glance told her who the woman was.

Sophie picked up the potted plant and swung it, smashing it against the man's head. The pot shattered. The man fell. Sophie went to Carla's aid, ripping the tape first from her mouth, then from her body.

Sophie pulled her X-Vid from her bag. "I'm calling the police."

The man was stirring. "Better get inside, first," said Carla.

As soon as they were safely inside the apartment, Carla locked the door.

Looking out the window, Sophie saw the man speed away in a hover. "He's gone," she said. "Do you still want me to call the police?"

"No point."

Carla put a kettle on but, seeing that her hands were shaking, Sophie took over. Carla sat on the couch while Sophie made tea.

"You've had a shock," said Sophie. "What you need is strong, sweet tea."

"Thanks, Sophie, but I don't take sugar."

"Now, tell me what that was all about." Sophie, handed Carla her tea. "Who was that horrible man?"

Carla shook her head. "I have no idea, but he wasn't my second date, if that's what you're thinking. What did you hit him with?"

"Oh, that was a houseplant I bought for you. I apologize."

Carla laughed. "No apology necessary."

"I came to tell you that Cassidy has turned up. He's in hospital."

Carla looked shocked. "What happened to him?"

"He fell off a roof somewhere near the docks. He's concussed. He broke an arm and a few ribs. One of them pierced his lung."

"That's terrible. I'll have to visit him."

"Better leave it for a few days. He's on a ventilator."

"Oh my god, Sophie, you must be worried."

"Tell me why that man had you all tied up. And where he was taking you?"

Carla sipped her tea. "It was lucky you turned up when you did. How did that happen?"

"Oh, I almost forgot, I was here to deliver a message from Cassidy. But tell me who that horrible man was first."

"What was Cassidy's message?"

176

"He said, 'Tell Carla not to trust Oscar. Oscar is a killer.'"

"Oscar is a killer? Are you sure that's what he said?"

"One hundred percent. Don't trust Oscar. Ooh, was that Oscar, that horrible man?"

Carla shook her head. "No, that wasn't Oscar."

Sophie listened as Carla explained that she and Cassidy had been working on a top secret development. Then Sophie frowned. "There was something else..."

"Something Cassidy said?"

"Yes..." The furrows on her brow deepened. She closed her eyes. "He said something about Oscar and the Southers... The Southers are going to take Oscar somewhere."

"To Leninets?"

Sophie shook her head. "No. I'm sorry I can't remember. Cassidy told me that your domestic servant lost a hand without feeling any pain. I told him about a similar genetic condition in humans. CIP, it's called. Is that what you were working on – making the androids feel pain? Is that why Cassidy disappeared?"

"That's what we've been working on, and I don't know why Cassidy disappeared. One of the AUs, the test subjects that we were working on, went missing, too. He was stolen from this apartment."

"Oscar?"

"Oscar."

Carla began to put the puzzle together. She was

certain then that the Southers had Oscar and they planned to move him to the D-System.

Sophie was working it out, too. "Oscar is a killer. Is that because of the pain you've given him?"

"Something like that," said Carla. "I think we can take it that Cassidy was taken against his will. He was injured trying to escape, and whoever took him tried to take me to replace him, now that he's in hospital."

"I'm not sure I follow all that," said Sophie, "but it seems to me that this apartment is no longer safe. You need to find somewhere else to live."

"You could be right," said Carla. "But where could I go?"

Chapter 36

"I know a place where you can go," said Sophie.

"Where?"

"ANTIX, the Resistance, have a hideout in the city. You'll be safe there for a while."

Carla was skeptical. "Why would they want to help? Aren't they opposed to the whole idea of androids?"

"I'm not sure about that, but they never fail anyone in trouble, and the leader's a friend of mine. He's a good man."

"What's his name, this good man?"

"Benn. He's a real charmer. You'll like him."

Carla woke Lia and told her to pack her kitbag. Lia reacted to the strange request with nothing but a flicker of the eyelids. "Just take two changes of clothes and all my underwear."

Carla put her precious computer and all her technical gear into a backpack.

The hovercab dropped them off at an address near the city center. "Is this it?" said Carla as the cab drove away.

Sophie said, "No, it's a few blocks away. We never let anyone know the exact address, for security reasons. I'm sure you understand."

"I understand," said Carla.

Sophie strode forward. "Come on, it's this way."

She took a circuitous route, stopping occasionally to make sure they weren't being followed, and reversing direction several times, giving Carla the feeling she had entered a world of spies and intrigue. Finally, Sophie stopped at a bland office block, a narrow building three stories high, surrounded by similar buildings. She gave three short and one long rings on the doorbell. The door opened and they stepped inside.

Sophie introduced Carla and Benn.

"Can I leave you two without a chaperone?" said Sophie. "I need to get back to the hospital."

Carla gave her a brief hug. "If he's awake, tell him I'll visit him as soon as I can."

Sophie gave Benn a peck on the cheek and headed off in search of a cab.

Benn was every bit as charming as Sophie had said. Carla liked the man; she couldn't help herself. She began by putting Lia's powerpack on recharge. Then she gave Benn a heavily edited version of her recent history.

"I was sorry to hear about Cassidy," he said. "I hope he's going to be all right. When you're finished your project, the android policemen will feel pain, is that right?"

The sparkle in his eyes showed he liked the idea of being able to inflict pain on Autonomic policemen.

"That's the plan, yes, and I'm close."

"What do you need?"

"I could use a few test subjects to experiment on. I can't keep using Lia."

"How many?"

"Six would be ideal."

Benn explained the aims of the Resistance. They were against the widespread exploitation of the physical assets of the colonies and the erosion of natural environments. His target list included a lot of modern inventions, with androids near the top of the list.

"Sounds like you want to move modern civilization back a thousand years," said Carla. "You're not one of those people who believe capitalism is evil?"

"Not at all," said Benn.

"So, it's the modern technology you object to?"

"Not really," he said. "We have no objection to progress as long as it doesn't destroy the environment or the natural ecosystems here on Earth or on any of the colonies."

"That's a tall order," she said.

"Yes, I accept that, but someone has to take a stand. Look at where the Earth was at the end of the twenty-first century before the discovery of Flor. The place was virtually uninhabitable. And all those problems, the pollution, the climate warming, the unforgiveable loss of so many animal species, the wars, the famines, even the pandemics, were all down to greed."

Carla couldn't disagree with any of that. It was a popular view of history.

"Which brings us to the main focus of our movement. Don't you agree that there is something inherently unsafe in placing so many key commodities and services in the hands of a single corporation?"

"You mean Xenodyne Industries?"

"The Great Monopoly, yes."

Again, Carla had to agree.

"You've seen how the police break up our protest marches?"

She nodded.

"A lot of the police in those cordons are androids."

"Is that an accusation?"

"No, Carla, it's a cry for help. Whatever chance we have against flesh and blood policemen, we have absolutely none against machines."

She was being maneuvered into a corner, and she knew it. "What can I do about that?"

"Help us to fight fire with fire."

Realization dawned. "You want AUs in the Resistance?"

He turned on his most charming smile. "We need our own android army, and I'm sure you can help us."

"An army? How many do you need?"

"A thousand would be a good round number, don't you think?" He beamed at her.

Carla shook her head, her mouth agape. "Do you want to start a war?"

"I'm hoping to avoid one."

"You're crazy," she said. "And anyway, I've no

idea where you could find anything like that number of AUs."

"I know a warehouse where they store lots of androids," he said.

#

It was a dark, moonless night. Carla looked up at the sky full of stars and picked out the constellation Aquarius, the location of the D-System where she thought her father might be. Eight of Benn's strongest men assembled, dressed in dark night-combat fatigues and climbed aboard a truck. Benn helped Carla into the cab. It was an antique, with wide rubber tires designed to run on the ground.

"I can't believe these things are still running," she said. "How old is it?"

"It's from the twenty-second century," he replied, turning the ignition key. The engine started with a throaty roar. "Listen to that. Doesn't it take you back?"

"Was it converted from fossil fuels?"

"Not this model, but it has an engine similar to the ones used to convert from diesel to electricity." He grinned and called out, "All set back there?"

Getting an answering *ra-tap* on the superstructure, he put the old monster into gear, and it juddered forward. Carla watched, fascinated, as Benn struggled with the gear lever. It was like something from an old silent movie!

"When we get there, I want you to hang back. If I need your help, I'll ask for it."

"Are the men armed?" she asked.

"No. I'm hoping no one will get injured. The plan is to subdue the guards, take what we came for and leave as quickly and as quietly as possible."

Chapter 37

They circled the city, keeping to the outer suburbs, and drew up outside a warehouse in an industrial area unfamiliar to Carla. Benn turned off the ignition and the old engine wound down. The men climbed out of the back of the truck and went into action.

Carla watched from the cab. Benn and his men entered the warehouse with ease. Then everything went quiet.

She was startled by a knock on the window. A figure shone a light in her eyes. She wound down the window.

"What is your business here?" said a patrolman, a Mark 5 Unit.

"I'm waiting for a friend," she said.

The patrolman circled the truck with his flashlight and returned to his starting point. "This is a very old vehicle," he said. "It shouldn't be on the road. Please step out, keeping your hands where I can see them."

Carla said, "Who am I?"

"You are Carla Scott."

"Yes, I am Carla Scott. I see no criminal activity,

here. You should continue on your way, patrolman, code one seven one five two three."

The patrolman tipped his cap. "Good night, Carla Scott," and he walked away.

A few more anxious minutes passed. Then Benn emerged from the building and climbed into the cab. "Everything is going according to plan," he said. "I'd like you to run your eyes over the androids before we take them, just to make sure they are fully functioning."

Carla climbed down and slipped inside the warehouse.

The lighting was subdued, but she caught sight of two guards in a monitoring station, trussed up and gagged in front of their security screens. Inside the warehouse she found stacks of shelving loaded with spare parts and, in one corner, rows and rows of XA Autonomic Units, some lying prone, others standing, all powered down.

"These are Mark 4 Units," she said.

"Does that mean we can't use them?" said Benn.

"You can use them, but they won't be a match for the latest models in a fight."

"Explain what you mean."

"The Mark 4 is obsolete. They aren't produced anymore. These Units will be sold into the domestic market or used as low-level workers. The Mark 5 Unit is faster, stronger; better in every way, really. The latest model, the Mark 6, is better again."

The expression on Benn's face showed his

disappointment. "Are you saying we shouldn't bother taking these androids?"

"Yes. I wouldn't bother."

He scratched his beard and gave the problem some thought. "Is there any way these Units could be enhanced? Could you help us to modify them to bring them up to the Mark 5 standard, say?"

"Not possible, I'm sorry."

"Is there nothing you can do to improve them?"

Carla gave that some thought. "It should be possible to build in some improvements, but I couldn't get them up to the level of the Mark 5 model. That's simply not possible."

"But you can make them better? Give them a half-decent chance in a fight against a Mark 5 police model?"

"Half-decent, maybe."

"Right, that's good enough for me." He ran off to organize the removal of the AUs.

They loaded the truck with 50 AUs and Benn took them back to the Resistance base. Carla rode back in the cab with him.

"How many did you take?"

"The truck could only take fifty. I'll go back for more once I've off-loaded these."

Carla was exhausted. She stumbled from the truck, found herself a cot in the women's dormitory and fell asleep right away.

#

"How many did you get?" she asked the next morning.

"Two hundred and seventy. It's a long way short of a thousand."

"Will it be enough?" she said.

"It'll have to be," replied Benn. "Now tell me what we need to bring them up to speed."

Carla inspected the haul. The building had a spacious basement where the men had stored the androids. They filled every available space, piled on top of each other like corpses after an air strike. Two of Benn's men helped her to extract four AUs and carry them up the stairs to a room at the back of the building that she'd picked out as her laboratory.

She opened her computer, established a link to the XA database and quickly uploaded the basic Mark 5 software. Then she installed powerpacks in the four AUs and downloaded as much as she could to two of them. Tests of a few critical functions proved that the upgraded Units were operating with improved functionally. She demonstrated the difference to Benn by setting all four AUs a series of simple tasks to perform – answering basic questions, moving around obstacles, catching objects thrown to them.

"Can they feel pain, now?" he asked.

"No, that function is still at the experimental stage."

"Okay. When will the police Units feel pain?" said Benn.

"Cassidy was working on it before his accident. I still have a lot to do to reproduce his work. When I have a software solution ready, it should be a simple matter to download it to all the Mark 5 and 6 Units, military and police. But at the moment it's a hardware function which would have to be manufactured and installed in the Autonomic population, one Unit at a time."

"Right, so not anytime soon?"

"Yes. But you should be aware that feeling pain and reacting to it in an appropriate manner are human traits. Autonomic Units that can do that will be better adapted to hostile situations, not worse."

"I can live with that," he said. "Just so long as we can make them feel pain."

Upon further inspection of the androids in the basement, Carla discovered a lone Popov buried under a pile of AUs. She had it transferred upstairs to her makeshift lab. Without a Souther powerpack, she couldn't power up the Unit, but she was able to tap into its code by connecting in through one of its access panels. A deep search of the data stored in the android's system revealed the address where it had been manufactured: 37 Walton. It was the best clue she had to where the Southers might be holding Alpha Oscar 113.

Chapter 38

When the Southers launched a fresh ground attack on the Los Angeles International Air- and Spaceport, in the early hours of Sunday morning, General F. C. Matthewson was called from his bed. Grumbling with exasperation he pulled on his fatigues, straightened his hat, put on his gloves, and headed for the helipad.

"They mean business this time, General," said Colonel Droppel. "At least two divisions have been seen to the north of LAX and one to the south. Our boys are holding their own for now, but I'm not optimistic. I fear we may lose the Ground Gate."

"Have you called in reinforcements?"

"Yes, sir. I've thrown every available android into the defense of the Spaceport."

The general gave the colonel a quizzical look as they climbed aboard the helihover.

"We haven't been able to fly in any men. The airport is unusable since the last artillery bombardment."

"Who's in charge?"

"Major Lasser is holding the northern line; the Marine Corps has the south. I'm not sure who's in command there."

The general slapped his thigh. "We can rely on the Marines to hold the line."

The helihover's rotors drowned out any further discussion, and the two men sat facing each other in silence as the aircraft transported them to the Spaceport.

As they approached LAX, the view from the helihover gave the general a bird's eye view of the battlefield. The troops to the north of the Spaceport were under pressure, but they were holding firm. The Marines to the south were well dug-in and dishing out as much flak as they were receiving.

"The Marines will hold," the general said, though no ears heard him.

Once they had hit the ground, and after the helihover had taken off, the general climbed into the waiting jeep. He straightened his hat. "I want you on the south side, Colonel. I'll take care of the north. Make radio contact as soon as."

The colonel saluted and hurried off to his station on foot. General Matthewson pointed north. "Take me to your leader, son," he said.

The jeep headed north, zigzagging around the rain-filled craters on the runways. The driver stepped on his brakes, raising a cloud of dust that found its way into the field headquarters of the northern defense line. General Matthewson saluted the young driver, made a half-hearted attempt to brush the dust from his uniform, straightened his hat, and entered the tent.

"Atten-shun! General on station," someone shouted.

Everyone in the tent sprang to attention. General Matthewson touched his hat with a gloved hand, "At ease, gentlemen." He picked out Major Lasser and approached him. "Give me a rapid sit-rep, Major."

The major obliged in just a few words. "We're seriously outnumbered, outgunned and out of options, General. The enemy is pressing hard. I have lost well over fifty percent of my fighting force. I doubt if we can stand for much longer."

"Use your artillery, man," said the general.

"I would, sir, but we've run out of shells."

"Send for more."

"I have, sir. We're waiting for them to arrive."

"When are they due?"

"What's today?"

"Sunday."

"They're due to arrive on Monday."

"Surely you can hold out until tomorrow?"

"No, sir, not tomorrow. That's Monday of next week."

The general's blood pressure rose a couple of notches. "You're telling me you've run out of artillery shells and fresh supplies won't arrive here for eight days?" The general removed his hat. "Get me a phone."

#

Colonel Droppel was having similar problems with the Marines defending the southern boundary of the Spaceport. Commander Gray was a career officer with a solid history of combat experience under his belt. One of the toughest Marines ever to graduate from the academy, commissioned in the field during the Second Lunar War, he knew his eggplant from his onions. And he knew a lost cause when he saw one.

"I'm sorry, Colonel. I've done everything humanly possible, but we will have to yield to them sooner than later. Without ammunition we have little choice."

"Couldn't you hold out a little longer?"

The commander shook his tousled head. "No point, sir. We would just lose more men for no gain."

The colonel found a radio operator. "Patch me through to General Matthewson at the northern defenses."

The radio operator obliged. He handed the instrument to the colonel.

"General, are you receiving?"

"Loud and clear. Go ahead, Droppel."

"The situation here is... fluid, sir," Droppel began.

"The Marines will hold," replied the general, firmly.

"Yes, sir. I mean no, sir, it doesn't look like it."

"What are you trying to say, Colonel? Spit it out, man."

"The outlook is bleak here, General. Commander Gray is short of ammunition. He has requested permission to surrender."

"What? You're breaking up, Colonel. Put the commander on the line."

Colonel Droppel gave the handset to Commander Gray, who straightened his back. "Commander Gray here, General."

"Report, Gray," said the general.

"The colonel gave you an accurate picture, sir. We held the position for as long as we could, but we've fired our last blast."

"Use your artillery, Commander."

"We have no shells left."

"What about mortars?"

"All mortar rounds are gone."

"Don't you have anything left?"

"No, sir. We could throw rocks at them. That's all we have."

"That's close to insubordination, soldier!"

"Yes, sir. Sorry, sir."

"Mount a counter-offensive." The general was shouting. "Use your androids."

The commander ran a sleeve across his face. "I wouldn't advise that, sir. Our Autonomics are... impulsive."

"What the hell does that mean, Commander? They are machines, are they not?"

"Yes, sir, but the Autonomics are the finest men we have. They will bravely follow any order I give them, but..."

"But what?"

"They are comrades in arms. You are asking me to place them under overwhelming enemy fire with nothing to defend themselves with."

The radio went ominously silent for a couple of moments.

"Are you refusing a direct order?"

Before the commander could answer that question, Colonel Droppel grabbed the phone from his hand. "Droppel here, General. The commander has gone to organize the counter-offensive."

"I'm very glad to hear it," said the general. "Keep me informed." He broke the connection.

Commander Gray glared at the colonel. "I have no intention of following that order."

Colonel Droppel led the commander out of earshot of the radio operator. "Yes, I know, but you were on the brink of destroying a long and distinguished career. I couldn't let you do that. You can report back that the counter-offensive was an abysmal failure, how you lost a high number of your Autonomics."

"I'll never get away with it," said the commander.

"Don't worry," said Droppel. "I'll cover for you. We should be able to massage the figures of android losses. It's not as if we have to come up with Marines in body bags. Now, start the withdrawal. I would suggest you move your men to the west. They may be able to evacuate by sea."

Chapter 39

Within minutes of the end of the radio conversation between General Matthewson and his two commanders, the Southers had broken through the Marines' defenses at the southern edge of the Spaceport and taken control of the vital Ground Gate. Fifteen minutes later, the defenders to the north had capitulated and the general was in a jeep, fleeing for his life toward the Pacific Ocean.

Once the enemy had control of the Spaceport, one battleship and a huge troop transport dropped from orbit through the Ground Gate, bolstering Souther troop and Popov numbers on the ground well beyond anything the Northers could muster.

The Northers responded by moving troops in from Mexico, Washington, Oregon and Nevada. The Southers sat tight, preparing for the coming confrontation. It was shaping up to be the biggest battle in the history of mankind since the Second Lunar War.

Again, the president of the Norther Federation Alliance made an impassioned speech on TV calling for restraint on both sides.

Not since the last Lunar War have so many men and machines faced each other with hostile intent. And in a highly populated area, where thousands of innocent bystanders would die. This battle must not take place. It would start a devastating war that neither side can win. A war of this magnitude would surely spread to the colonies. There would be no winners. Both sides would lose, and unthinkable numbers of civilians would perish. Mankind would lose everything gained over the past three hundred years. Is this to be the legacy of our generation? Is this what the leaders of our respective peoples worked together to create? Is this what so many of the pioneer captains of the early spaceships gave their lives for? What will we build for our great grandchildren?

The corresponding speech by the premier of the Souther Federation Bloc, no less impassioned, demanded a climb down from the Northers. He attacked the elitist privilege of the Northers, backing his claims with statistics, comparing North and South. The average lifespan for Southers across all Six Systems was four standard years lower than for Northers, the infant mortality and unemployment rates were higher, the cumulative wealth of the Northers was nearly twenty percent higher. And of the ten colonized planets in the Six Systems, only the three, those in the D-System, were controlled by the Southers.

The late-night news reported that tentative

discussions had reopened between the two parties. No one in the ANTIX safehouse was optimistic about the outcome of the talks.

While the Resistance workers were absorbed by the TV coverage, Carla spent her time adjusting the code in Lia's fear module. Her intention was to provide Lia's learning algorithm with a method to overcome irrational fears. It was no more than a shot in the dark, but she reckoned it should give Lia a chance to work her way out of her phobia, given enough time.

#

Carla went to the communal area to turn on the TV first thing the next day. Benn and several of his team had beaten her to it.

The newscaster could barely contain his excitement. A tentative ceasefire had been agreed. The president and the premier had met in person to ratify the agreement. As a goodwill gesture, the cargo lost from the *Vladivostok* in the AD Conduit would be replaced by the Norther Alliance. A second Souther freighter, the *Archangel*, would take an alternate, slower route from Earth to the D-System through two Conduits, AC and CD. As an additional safeguard, the freighter would be accompanied by a fleet of Norther fighters.

Both armies were stood down, holding their positions. Benn and his team applauded the good news. Carla joined in. The Six Systems were safe for the moment.

Chapter 40

Carla and Benn accompanied Sophie on her visit to the hospital. Cassidy was in a coma, on a ventilator and connected to a bewildering array of bleeping monitors. Carla and Sophie spoke with a nurse.

"You'd need to talk to the doctor, but I can tell you he's had a nasty knock to the head. We are hopeful that he will make a full recovery, of course, but it could go either way. The doctor will be here in about two hours. As I said, you would need to talk with him."

Carla sat with the patient for a few minutes, then she gave Sophie a hug and left with Benn.

On the way to the hoverpark, she told Benn that an examination of the enemy android code had given her the address of a Souther base where she might find her missing AU. "I'm going to need help getting him back."

"His name is Oscar, if I'm not mistaken," said Benn.

"Alpha Oscar 113, to be precise," she replied.

"Why is it so important to recover this particular Unit?" he asked.

"He's been held by the Southers for over two weeks. I'm sure they have been interfering with his code. An investigation of his code could reveal a lot about what their engineers are planning."

"Very well," said Benn. "We'll go tonight, as soon as it gets dark."

#

They decided not to use a vehicle; 37 Walton was no more than six blocks from the Resistance safehouse. Benn chose two of his best men for the mission. Carla and Lia left through the front door. Benn and his men waited a few minutes before leaving through the rear entrance. They all reassembled a few blocks from the safehouse and made their way to the Souther base.

A sliver of a new moon lit their path. Carla had no idea what they might encounter there. She hoped she might find a research lab, but it could be nothing more than a storage area.

No. 37 Walton was a blocky 3-story building with dormer windows overlooking the bay. As they approached the building, Lia reached out to Oscar. She got no answer.

"We need to get inside," said Carla. "What's the plan?"

Benn said, "We'll create a diversion round the back. You go in through the front door."

Carla and Lia found a shady spot to hide on the opposite side of the road. They didn't have long to wait. A plume of smoke rose into the sky from behind the building. Within seconds, the front door flew open and people began to emerge. At the same time, three hovers shot out from the rear of the building. All three headed off in different directions.

"Wait here, Lia." Carla headed off toward the building.

She was halfway across the road when Lia called her back, "I have made contact with Oscar. He is in a hover going west."

Carla hurried back to Lia. "Ask him to stay in contact as long as he can. Tell him we need to know where he finishes his journey."

Lia said, "He is turning north... Now east, now north..."

Carla ran around to the rear of the building. She found Benn and his men concealed behind some large dumpsters.

"Oscar is in one of those hovers," she said. "We need to go after him."

"Do you know where he's going?"

"Not yet, but he's heading north."

They ran back to the Resistance base where Benn grabbed a hover and Carla and Lia climbed aboard.

"Where is he now?" said Carla.

"Oscar is approaching Los Angeles airport..."

Benn accelerated.

As they approached the airport, Lia said, "Oscar is no longer transmitting."

Carla swore. "They are taking him off-world. They must be going to place him on that freighter bound for the D-System. Once that ship leaves, we'll never see Oscar again."

They were prevented from entering the airport by an armed guard of Souther troops. "Move along," said one of the guards. "The airport is out of commission until further notice."

Benn took the hover to the boundary fence where they could see what was going on at the Spaceport. Every few minutes a monster hovertruck arrived fully laden to be off-loaded near the Ground Gate before leaving empty. Stevedores driving forklifts then moved the off-loaded freight into covered shuttle bays. As they watched, they heard a shuttle's engines fire up and die abruptly. This was the telltale sign that a shuttle full of cargo had entered the Ground Gate. Within minutes it would emerge from the Orbital Gate, dock with the massive freighter, the *Archangel*, waiting in stationary orbit in space, and transfer its cargo.

"That's the end of the line, I guess," said Benn.

"Not necessarily," Carla replied.

Chapter 41

She called Stepan on her X-Vid. She got a busy signal. "Hi Carla, sorry I can't take your call right now. Please leave a message."

"Call me back as soon as you get this, Stepan. It's urgent."

"What do we do next?" said Benn.

"You go back to base," said Carla. "Lia and I will keep watch here. If we can reconnect with Oscar, we may still be able to recover him."

Benn was reluctant to leave Carla alone so close to a Souther stronghold.

"I'll be fine. I'm not alone. I have Lia," said Carla.

Benn gave her his X-Vid number and left. Carla found a café not far from the airport. She took an outside table with a view of the Spaceport and ordered a coffee. The waitress that served her was an Autonomic Unit. Carla recognized an early Mark 4 AU, not the brightest model ever produced, but smart enough to take an order and get it to the right table without spilling anything.

"What about your friend?" said the waitress.

Lia gave her a withering look.

Carla said, "My friend doesn't drink coffee."

"Would she prefer tea? Or fruitoid? We do a selection of fruitoid juices." She handed Lia a menu.

"No thank you, my friend is not thirsty," said Carla, and the waitress left.

Carla kept a watch on the trucks arriving and departing. She estimated the time between deliveries and the tonnage in each truck. The first freighter that had gone missing was carrying three million tons of cargo. Based on that, and her estimates of times of arrival and tons per load, she calculated that this freighter would be full and ready to depart in under a week.

"Keep trying to reach Oscar," she said to Lia. "I need to know where he is."

The coffee, when it arrived, was lukewarm. Carla smiled at the waitress and thanked her. She scuttled off to annoy the people at another table.

Stepan rang. "Hi Carla, what do you need?"

"Where are you?"

"I'm at work. You said it was urgent."

"Yes, could we meet? I'm at the Plate and Bowl. It's near—"

"I know where it is. I have fifteen minutes. I'll be there in five. Order me a Luna Special White."

Carla signaled to the waitress and ordered Stepan's drink. It arrived in double quick time. The waitress put the coffee on the table in front of Lia. "Enjoy." She 'smiled' sweetly.

Lia looked at her blankly. Carla said, "Thank

you." And the waitress scurried away.

When Stepan arrived, he looked at his watch. "I can give you five minutes, no longer. We're shuttling a large cargo up to a freighter in orbit, the *Archangel*."

"Where's the freighter going?" she asked.

He raised an eyebrow. "She's heading to the D-System. You remember that ship that was lost? This one will replace it."

"We saw that on the TV news," said Lia.

"What can I do for you, Carla?"

"We need to get on board that freighter."

Stepan's mouth fell open. "Why on earth would you want to go to the D-System?"

"Never mind why. Can you get us on board?"

Ten seconds passed before he responded. "I suppose it could be arranged. How many people are we talking about?"

"Just me and Lia."

Stepan looked at Lia.

"She's my personal Autonomic Unit. You remember her."

"I remember. She lost an arm."

"That was a hand. Can you help us?"

He checked his watch again. "I have to go. Leave it with me. I'll see what can be arranged."

"When is the *Archangel* due to leave?"

He drained his coffee and stood up. "She leaves tomorrow at noon. You will need to meet me here three hours before that. Bring a single bag. You'll need winter clothing. It gets pretty cold in the

Conduits." He looked at Lia again. "Just one bag. I assume your... Lia won't need a change of clothes."

#

At 10 a.m. the following day, Carla and Lia were sitting at the same table in the same café waiting for Stepan to appear.

"Stepan is late," said Lia.

Carla searched Lia's face for signs of impatience. She saw none, but there was something odd about the way Lia was sitting, slightly hunched, as if prepared to leap forward at a moment's notice.

"He'll be here soon enough," said Carla. "Have you heard anything from Oscar?"

"No."

"Keep trying. I need to know that he's definitely on that freighter before we board."

Stepan arrived at 10:30, looking uncomfortable. "I've set it up so that I can smuggle you onto a shuttle. You'll have to spend the journey inside a cargo bay on the *Archangel*. I'm sorry, but that's the best I could do at such short notice."

"That will be fine," said Carla. "How long is the journey to the D-System?"

"From here to the C-System is 21 hours. From C to D is another 300 hours. That's 12 and a half days."

"So I'll need food for 14 days," said Carla. Her stomach did a cartwheel. Two weeks in a cargo bay was a daunting prospect.

"You will be sharing the cargo bay with about fifty thousand tons of Pexcorn Foods protein blocks. You could chew on that."

"What about water?"

"That won't be a problem. There's water on faucet in every cargo bay. There's a toilet, too, but it's pretty basic."

"Will I be exposed to open space at any time during the transfer from the shuttle to the cargo bay?"

He shook his head. "The shuttle will dock fully with the *Archangel*. All you have to do is slip from one to the other while the shuttle crew are transferring their load."

She nodded.

"You're sure you want to do this?" he said. "The D-System colonies are not the most hospitable of places."

"Not yet," said Carla. "I'm hoping for confirmation before we reach the point of no return."

He looked at his watch again. "That would be in about seventeen minutes."

Chapter 42

Lia and Carla climbed aboard Stepan's hover. He covered them with a blanket. "Stay quiet until I tell you it's safe."

The hover set off. Carla heard Stepan pass through two security checks before it came to a halt.

Stepan removed the blanket. He led them through a door and closed it. "You can hide in here until I come and get you."

Carla looked around her. They were in a cramped space with a low ceiling, surrounded by piles of tarpaulins and coils of rope. Her nose wrinkled from an acrid smell that filled the room.

Stepan grinned. "That's tar from the ropes. You get used to it."

"Where are we?" she said.

"It's a storeroom in one of the loading bays. There's a shuttle right outside. Stay quiet. I'll tell you when to move, all right?"

The Stepan she knew was gone. The Stepan who was her boyfriend for nearly three years was a gentle soul; this man was a hard-nosed competent operator, a go-getter. She was sure he'd done this sort of thing before – and probably for money.

He left through a second door on the opposite side of the room.

A half hour went by. The smell of tar became increasingly suffocating and nauseating. Carla tried breathing through her mouth, but the choking sensation persisted.

Lia tried to contact Oscar every few minutes, but without success. Then Stepan came back in through the second door.

"All set? It's time to go."

"Give us a minute," said Carla. "Lia, try Oscar once more."

Lia closed her eyes for a moment.

She shook her head. "No."

"It's time," said Stepan. "Do you want to go? Last chance to change your mind."

Carla picked up her kitbag. "Lead on."

"You've been through a Gate before?"

"When I was ten. I remember it wasn't pleasant."

"It's a jolt, but it won't do you any harm. You'll hear the warning signal. The transit from Ground to Orbit takes just a few minutes. When the shuttle docks with the *Archangel* you'll have to find your own way from one to the other. It shouldn't be difficult."

Stepan took them through the second door and straight into the cargo bay of a shuttle. He closed the cargo bay doors. Carla was surrounded by hundreds of pallets of protein blocks in 5-high tiers.

The first jolt when they entered the Ground Gate came as a shock, without any warning. It shook Carla more than she had expected. She looked at Lia. The AU seemed unaffected, perhaps even unaware of what had happened.

She was better prepared for the second jolt when the shuttle emerged through the Orbital Gate. But suddenly they were in zero gravity. She had to hold on to the pallets. Lia did the same. The conventional engines fired up with a roar and she felt the smooth acceleration as they moved through normal space. The only sensations she felt as they docked with the larger ship were a deceleration followed by the powering down of the engines. The artificial gravity from the larger freighter put them back on their feet. After that, there was absolute silence for a few minutes; all she could hear was her own breathing and faint rustling from her own clothing.

The cargo bay doors opened and an operator on a forklift began to transfer the pallets of protein from the shuttle to the *Archangel*. It was an easy matter to slip across without being seen and hide in the walkway between two rows 100 pallets long and 10 high.

Once the last pallet had been transferred across, the forklift operator paused to relieve himself in the toilet cabinet before closing the access panel doors. The shuttle withdrew. A few minutes after that, the engines of the *Archangel* fired up and Carla felt a sensation of acceleration. About 30 minutes later, the engines died.

She asked Lia to try contacting Oscar one more time before putting her to sleep to conserve her power. Lia failed to make contact. A wave of panic washed over Carla. *What if Oscar is not on board?*

A piercing klaxon sounded. Too late to change her mind now! Carla braced herself for the jolt and the *Archangel* entered the Gate to the AC Conduit.

Over the following few hours, the temperature fell steadily. Carla put on her warm clothes. She inspected the toilet. It was barely adequate and not too clean, but it would have to do. Pulling a dozen boxes of protein from a pallet, she fashioned a seat for herself from them. Her stomach was rumbling loudly before she began to eat the small amount of food she'd brought with her. The faucet that Stepan had promised produced a trickle of brown, murky water.

After 12 hours, the temperature in the cargo bay fell below freezing. Carla was having difficulty keeping her teeth from rattling in her head. She added some more protein boxes to make a bed for herself and lay down, covering her legs with the rest of the warm clothing from her kitbag.

She slept on and off for a few hours and woke up hungry again. Breaking open one of the boxes, she clawed some protein from a block of frozen protein and wrapped it in a warm sweater until it was thawed enough to eat. It tasted like mold, but she was grateful that it wasn't too hard to break with her teeth. She washed it down with some murky water. Then she spent an hour doing exercises. She had to keep her body in shape. Without exercise her muscles would atrophy and the cold could kill her.

The klaxon woke her. The jolt shook her to the core as the *Archangel* left the AC Conduit Gate and entered the C-System. Her birthplace! A ridiculous twinge of nostalgia struck her, and thoughts of her mother and her estranged father brought unexpected tears to her eyes. Her fingers sought the comfort of her father's lighter in her pocket.

She woke Lia. "See if you can contact Oscar," she said. It was a forlorn hope, but she had to try.

Lia closed her eyes, then opened them again. "Oscar is on the ship."

That news was such a relief! Carla breathed a huge sigh.

"Do you know where he is?"

"No, but he is safe."

The freighter's conventional engines fired up, and Carla gazed out the porthole at the magnificent sight of Califon, her home planet, floating like a desert island in space below them, her two moons standing guard behind her. After 30 minutes, the engines died, the klaxon sounded again, and they entered the CD Gate. Carla knew from that point on she was facing 12 days of cold and unrelenting boredom. She did what she could to make her bed more comfortable...

Chapter 43

Searching among the endless pallets of protein blocks, Carla found a store of energy bars. The carbohydrates and nuts were welcome.

She turned her thoughts to the mole. Who could have stolen her code and passed it to the Southers? Major Grant sprang to mind immediately. He knew nothing about android software or hardware, but he had access to every part of the building, and he was creepy enough to be working for the enemy. Ricarda Petrik was another who had access, and Fritz Franck, of course. But the obvious candidate was her assistant, Cassidy. He'd reacted with shock when he'd seen her code in the Popov. Could his reaction have been artificial? If it was, then his acting skills were worthy of a career in Hollywood.

She continued her exploration of the cargo bay and came across a corner where the workmen had congregated during the long-drawn-out loading process. There were old half-empty coffee cups, a dog-eared pack of playing cards and a portable TVid set. Gathering the playing cards together, she took them back to her lair. She could play solitaire. And perhaps when she got really desperate, she could wake Lia and teach her to play gin rummy.

There were 49 cards in the pack. She returned to the workmen's cubbyhole and searched for the missing cards. She found the ace of diamonds, torn in half. Reducing the pack to three suits and reinventing a 39-card version of solitaire kept her busy for a couple of hours. After that, she struggled to sleep in the cold.

Keeping careful track of time was important for her sanity, and she did her best, but after a while she began to wonder if she'd lost track already. The TVid was no help as it had no access to current news channels. She watched half of an old movie that she'd seen years earlier. Had it only been three days and nights since they'd entered the CD Gate? It felt longer. She began to doubt that she could survive another nine days with not contact with humanity and without her music. She cursed the lack of a recharging station in the cargo bay. Lia would have been a great help to her in the isolation and boredom of her situation.

On day four she began to watch the news archives on the TVid. Diligently, she paged through story after story, everything a week or more old. She read of economists' doomsday warnings, celebrity sexual misconduct and marriage breakdowns, petty legal cases in different parts of the Six Systems, and advertisements for women's clothing and fruitoid concoctions. Then she discovered a small item at the bottom of a page dated nine days prior to departure.

PETRIK PLEADS GUILTY

The well-known investment fund manager, Hercules Petrik has pleaded guilty to 37 sample charges of securities fraud. The former chairman and CEO of Petrik Squares, an investment fund with an estimated 15,000 clients based in every colony of the 5 western Systems, has confessed to leading a large financial fraud. The fraud was worth well in excess of $17 million at current market prices. Many of Petrik's clients are reported to have lost their homes and their businesses. Petrik was born on Liberté in the C-System. Famously, he left school at the age of 14 (standard) and began his career as a shoeshine boy in the streets of East Chicag. His wife, the socialite Ricarda Petrik, a full board member of Xenodyne Industries is not implicated in the scheme.

Carla re-read the article several times in utter amazement. She imagined the rumor mill in the office working overtime. What could this mean for

Ricarda? Would she lose her position as CFO of Xenodyne Automation?

#

Fritz Franck was under pressure. Calls had been coming in daily from his military contacts, demanding updates on all outstanding projects. He had been able to respond with updates for projects in the Structural and Materials teams, but he had heard nothing for weeks from the two main development projects under Carla Scott's control.

"The listening device in the lab has picked up nothing for three weeks," said Major Grant.

"Which means she hasn't been at work."

Grant shrugged. "She may have found the device and removed it."

"Get over there and check it out. What are we paying you for?"

"If I find her, do you want me to tell her to report to you?"

Franck waved a dismissive hand. "Just find her. I want to know where she is. And see if you can find her assistant."

Major Grant started his search in Carla Scott's lab. The place was deserted. He checked his listening device. It was undisturbed and working. Next, he took his hover to Carla Scott's apartment. There was no one home. The neighbors were no help.

He returned to Xenodyne Automation and

The *Archangel* responded:

PERMISSION GRANTED

When the pirates crashed through onto the bridge, the XO and the bridge crew fired their blasters. Nothing happened. The pirates were carrying antique handguns. They fired back, and three crewmen fell.

The captain ordered his men to lower their weapons. The XO and the crew dropped their blasters.

Two fighter pilots rushed to the bridge and were cut down mercilessly by the pirates.

"Put down your weapons," the captain called out.

And the *Archangel* was taken.

#

Watching through the porthole, Carla saw the fighters zoom past. She couldn't see where they were going, but she knew a space battle was unfolding. She woke Lia.

"Come on, Lia. It's time we announced our presence."

She repacked her kitbag. Then she opened the internal airlock. They both got inside, and she opened the second door. They were met by a tall man in a strange costume – a short tunic adorned with brass buttons in two parallel rows. His hair hung like greasy tendrils over his shoulders.

"Where are you off to, my lovely?" He flashed a toothless smile.

There was a whiff of something putrid about him. His hand rested on the butt of a gun that looked like a 6-shooter from the wild west of nineteenth century USA.

"We need to speak with the captain."

"We? Oh, you mean you and your mechano companion?" He chuckled. "What's her name?"

"Let us pass," said Carla.

The man stood aside, which surprised Carla and gave her an indication of the direction she needed to go. She hurried on. Lia followed a couple of steps behind, carrying the kitbag, and the man followed a few steps behind Lia.

Carla was pretty sure what had happened. The *Archangel* was in the hands of a band of pirates. The thought of what the loss of another fully laden freighter would do to the fragile peace nauseated her. A calamitous war would surely follow and consume the Earth and all her colonies.

Chapter 45

They came to the end of the cargo bays and passed through the crew quarters. A sign on the wall pointed to the bridge.

Lia stopped suddenly. The pirate poked her. "What you stoppin' for?"

Lia said, "Oscar has contacted me." There was a tremor in her voice.

"Ask Oscar if he knows where he is," said Carla.

"He is in the crew quarters."

"We need to go back."

"I don't think so," said the pirate. "Keep moving." He pulled the gun from his belt and waved it at Carla.

Carla said, "Lia..."

Lia took a step toward the man and grabbed the barrel of his gun before he could pull the trigger. She wrenched it from his grasp and handed it to Carla.

The man gave a howl of indignation like a slighted schoolboy. He lunged at Carla. Lia held him back with one arm.

Carla pointed the gun at the pirate. "Lead us back to the crew quarters."

The pirate turned and led them back the way they'd come. It took Lia 30 standard seconds to find Oscar standing among the hammocks in the crew sleeping quarters.

"Hello Oscar," said Carla.

"Hello Carla Scott."

"Hello Oscar," said Lia. Carla imagined a warmth in her voice. Pure imagination, of course.

"Hello Lia."

"Now that everyone is fully acquainted, can we get on?" said the pirate.

A movement in the gloom at the back of the room caught Carla's eye. "Who's back there?"

Three men emerged. "Don't shoot," said one. "We're crew. We got separated and cut off from the rest when the pirates came."

"Where are the rest of the crew?" said Carla.

"The pirates took them away."

"Find some rope," she said. "Tie this one up."

"You don't want to do this," said the smelly pirate. "You'll be sorry."

"Stick something in his mouth while you're at it," she said.

While the other two crewmen tied up the pirate and gagged him, Carla asked their leader his name.

"Dmitri."

"Did you wake my Autonomic Unit?"

"He's yours is he?"

"Yes. His name's Oscar. Do you have any weapons, Dmitri?"

"We have our blasters, but they don't work inside the Conduit. We have no defense against their bullets."

"How many crew members are there?"

"There were twelve men and eight Popovs when we set out, but we lost three crewmen and two Popovs when the pirates took the ship."

"So there are six crew somewhere on the ship?"

Dmitri shook his head. "They are all locked up. There's just us three."

"We'll have to avoid the Popovs," said Carla. "They may be hostile toward us."

Oscar said, "I have contacted them. They are friendly, but they speak very little English."

Carla was stunned by this development. No Autonomic Unit had ever communicated with an enemy Popov before. She assumed this was as a result of the time he'd spent in a Souther lab.

"Ask them to join us. Tell them I intend to recapture the ship."

#

Three Popovs from the crew were soon gathered together in the crew's sleeping quarters. They were a miserable looking bunch of low-functioning deckhands designed for swabbing the decks, lifting and carrying, and other menial tasks.

Carla took charge. "We will storm the bridge and take back the ship. The pirates have old-fashioned weapons. We have none, but we are stronger than them. Now tell me you can take them."

Dmitri translated.

The response she got was half-hearted. "What's the matter with you guys?" she said.

One of the crew said something. Dmitri translated. "Their powerpacks are depleted. This one is at forty percent, this one is below thirty."

"This one is below ten," said another crewman.

"Never mind," said Carla. "We will just have to do the best we can with what we have. Are you with me, men?"

Dmitri translated.

The response was a lackluster "*Da.*"

Carla led the way to the bridge. Oscar followed close behind. Lia picked up Carla's kitbag and followed Oscar and the Popovs followed her. The three crew members took up the rear. As they approached the bridge, Oscar pushed ahead of Carla. She called out to him to wait, but he ignored her; clearly, the AU had built up a head of steam. He shattered the door and barged through onto the bridge. The captain of the *Archangel* was in his chair, looking close to apoplexy. The pirate chief stood behind the captain, in conversation with a tall, thin man with a strong head of hair and dark, bushy eyebrows.

When Oscar saw the tall man, he charged. The pirate chief fired his handgun, hitting Oscar plumb in his chest plate. The Popovs flooded in and were met with a hail of bullets from an automatic pistol in the hands of a pirate to their left. Two of the Popovs went down immediately.

The three crew members rushed in. Dmitri was hit and fell. Lia placed her body in front of Carla, protecting her. She was hit. Her body spun around and she staggered away, exposing Carla to the gunman. As she fell, and before the second pirate could fire his pistol at Carla, Lia launched the kitbag at him, knocking him to the deck. He toppled backward and the pistol flew from his hands.

Oscar roared and kept going. The pirate chief fired again, hitting Oscar in the left eye. Still Oscar wouldn't go down, but the loss of one of his cameras disrupted his spatial sense and the blow with his fist that should have killed the tall man glanced off his chest instead. Finally, Oscar lost his balance, stumbled and fell. His body twitched once and stopped moving.

One of the crewmen picked up the automatic pistol and leveled it at the pirate chief. The pirate chief responded by pulling the freighter captain from his chair, wrapping his arm around the neck, and pointing his handgun at his head. "Drop the weapon or your captain dies," he snarled.

Everyone froze. The crewman threw the pistol to the deck and the second pirate scrambled across on his knees to pick it up.

The battle was over. Their attempt to retake the *Archangel* had failed.

"Nice try, Madam," said the pirate captain. He

released the freighter captain. "What's your name?"

Carla gave him no answer.

The thin man pointed a finger at her. "That's Carla Scott, the Norther Federation's top android whisperer."

"What does that mean?"

"She's their number one android engineer."

"Lock them up," said the pirate chief.

Carla glanced at Oscar, lying immobile on the deck and then at Lia, clutching her left arm. She pulled Lia close. "I need to check these two Units," she said, dropping to her knees beside Oscar.

"You and you," said the pirate chief to two of his men. "Leave the woman and the dead mechanos. Take the rest below."

Two armed pirates rose from their operating stations and pushed Lia, the crewmen, and the surviving Popov toward the door. Dmitri struggled to his feet and he left, propped up between the other two crewmen.

Carla was left with an immobile Oscar. "I'd like to take him somewhere to inspect the damage," she said, not expecting a positive response.

"Help her," said the pirate chief to the man with the automatic pistol. "Take them both and lock them up."

Carla picked up her kitbag on the way out.

Chapter 46

They locked Carla in a cabin. Oscar lay on the floor with a neat round hole in his breast panel. A wave of anxiety swept over her as she removed the panel. Inside, she found his core processor dangling on the end of a couple of cables. It had been dislodged from its mounting and several of its cable connectors had popped out. The processor appeared undamaged. She replaced it on its mountings and reconnected it.

The second bullet had shattered Oscar's left camera. Removing a smaller access panel on the side of his head, she assessed the damage. The camera had been pushed deep into his cranial cavity, destroying the links between his vision and his Orientation module. There was nothing else between his ears apart from his audio processing equipment.

She initiated Oscar's start-up sequence.

He opened his one remaining eye.

"Can you see me?" she asked.

"I see you."

His right eye was still functioning.

"Can you hear me?" she asked.

"I hear you."

"Your hearing hasn't failed," she said, relieved.

"Please repeat the question."

Carla laughed. Had Oscar made a joke?

She checked him over and discovered that one of his knees was bent at a strange angle.

"What happened to your knee, Oscar?"

"I fell from the roof."

"Was that the same roof that Cassidy fell from?"

"Cassidy was on the roof. I fell."

"You didn't see Cassidy fall?"

No response.

"Who was that man on the bridge?" she said.

"Igor."

"Tell me what you know about Igor," she said.

"Igor is a Souther engineer. He gave me much pain."

She looked around the cabin for anything that she could use as a weapon. She found nothing. The door was locked.

"See if you can reach Lia."

Oscar said, "I have spoken with Lia. She is with one Souther Unit."

"Only one?"

"There are five, but four have no power."

Carla's anxiety had increased. Her heart was pounding, and her hands had developed a tremor. It was a feeling she remembered from when her mother had left her father, years earlier. This time her anxiety was about Lia. She needed to be reunited with Lia as soon as possible.

#

Captain Blackmore looked askance at Igor. "That android really wanted to kill you. Any idea why?"

Igor shrugged. "I have no idea. I thought it wanted to attack you,"

"I don't think so. I've never seen a mechano so intent on attacking a human. Are you sure you don't know why?"

"I'm certain."

"In that case it can be discarded like the rest."

"Discarded? What do you mean? Don't you keep them?"

"Mechanos are no use to us. We remove their powerpacks and eject them into space."

"Listen, Captain." Igor swallowed hard. "That android, the one with Carla Scott, is not like any other. I have been working with it. It's a prototype of a new military Unit. If you keep it safe, the Souther Federation will pay you to deliver it to the D-System."

The pirate chief's eyes narrowed. "How much?"

"You could name your price."

"So, it's not just another mechano?"

"It's a special Unit."

"And I could name my price?"

"Yes."

#

The smelly pirate was discovered by his mates and freed from his bonds amid much jocularity. "What happened, Barnrat? I heard you were tied up by a woman?"

"I was tied up by three crewmen and two androids."

"But a female android took your gun?" The pirate put an arm across the smelly man's shoulders.

Barnrat shrugged him off and headed to the bridge, the crewmen's laughter ringing in his ears.

#

When the freight had been secured, Captain Blackmore signaled to one of his lieutenants. "It's time to dispose of the androids. Eject them all, but keep the one with the female engineer." He turned to his other lieutenant. "And you, Barnrat, put the captain with his crew. We'll decide what to do with them later. And take this skinny one with you." He pointed a bony finger at Igor.

"I thought we had a deal, Captain," said a wide-eyed Igor.

"I don't make deals with the likes of you. Take them both away."

"What should I do with the woman?" said Barnrat.

Blackmore returned an evil, toothless grin. "Eject her with her beloved androids."

PART 5 – WAR

Chapter 47

The cabin door opened, and Barnrat, the putrescent pirate, came in. The handgun in his fist was cocked and ready to fire.

"Come with me," he said. "Leave the mechano."

Oscar made a move to get to his feet, but Carla told him to stay where he was.

She had to squeeze past the pirate in the doorway.

"Just give me an excuse," he said, his rancid breath washing over her face.

She held her kitbag up to her chest between them. "I don't want any trouble."

He locked Oscar in the cabin and led Carla to one of the cargo bays, where she found Lia and eight Popovs, six of them immobile, their powerpacks depleted. Lia looked exhausted. Carla checked her powerpack. It was down to 17 percent.

"You should rest to conserve your power," said Carla.

Lia shook her head. "I am afraid, Carla. The pirates will throw us out of the cargo bay doors."

"Nonsense," said Carla. "Why would they throw away such valuable merchandise?"

"Oscar has spoken with the Popovs. They say the pirates removed the powerpacks and threw out the crew of other ships."

Carla shivered. If they opened the cargo bay doors to eject Lia and the Popovs, she would die with them. She would hate to die in space, but she would regret the loss of her friend even more. And more than anything, she now regretted giving Lia the dubious gift of fear.

She checked Lia's wound. The bullet had entered her upper arm and gone right through. There were entry and exit wounds, but the damage looked superficial.

"How does it feel, Lia?"

"I have pain. I will live," Lia answered.

The internal airlock opened, and a lone pirate came in. Carla got the shock of her life when she saw him.

"Father? Is that you? How...?"

He had lost a lot of weight. His tunic and pants hung loosely around his frame, and his hair was almost pure white, but it was definitely him.

"Come quickly, Carla," he said. "I'll explain later. Follow me."

Carla grabbed her kitbag. She and Lia climbed into the airlock with her father. He opened the internal door and led them down a corridor past rows and rows of internal cargo bay doors. Then he stopped, said, "Wait here," and disappeared into a cargo bay.

He emerged with the *Archangel*'s captain and his entire crew, as well as Igor, the lanky Souther. "I have a ship waiting," he said. "I'm hoping you and your crew will know how to operate it, Captain."

"What sort of ship is it, Commissioner?" said the captain of the *Vladivostok*.

"I don't know. All I can tell you is that it is very old, and it's called the *Missie Bess*. It's this way."

"Wait," said Carla. "I can't leave without Oscar."

"Who's Oscar?" said her father.

"Never mind. You go ahead, leave Lia with me. We'll join you when we have Oscar."

"I'm not leaving without you," said her father.

"You won't have to. Now, go."

The men all followed Carla's father. Carla told Lia to talk to Oscar. "Tell him where we are. Tell him to come and find us."

"He is out of the cabin," said Lia after a moment. "He is running. His leg is damaged." Then, "He has reached the cargo area." And, "He has stopped. The pirates are shooting at him."

"Come on, Lia. He needs our help." Carla broke into a sprint.

Carla and Lia dashed back toward the crew quarters. Soon, they heard shots. Carla took cover in an open internal airlock. "Ask Oscar to give you an update."

Lia said, "He is pinned down. They fire at him every time he moves."

"Tell him to stay hidden." She looked around for something – anything – she could use to create a diversion. She touched her father's lighter in her pocket and had an idea. She tore off Lia's modacrylic shirt and set it alight. Acrid black smoke filled the corridor. Soon, two coughing pirates emerged from their hiding places, and Lia went into action. Taking a flying leap, she landed on the first man's kneecap. Carla jumped onto the back of the second man. She recognized his smell. She grappled with the man as he tried to turn his gun on her. It took all her strength to keep the gun pointing away. Then Oscar arrived. He grabbed the man by the back of his collar, lifted him off his feet, smashed him off the bulkhead and dumped him onto the floor, where he lay still. Carla picked up the gun and all three ran to the cargo bay where her father and the crew were waiting.

They piled inside. The door closed. Captain Korskov gave the order to disengage and moved the *Missie Bess* away from the freighter. Then he turned the craft around and set it moving back toward the C-System.

Chapter 48

Running on her silent Brazill Drive, the *Missie Bess* headed back the way she'd come through the CD Conduit to the C-System. The temperature was just below freezing throughout the old ship. Carla dressed Lia in one of her warm sweaters before putting Lia and Oscar on recharge. Then Carla and her father had a private meeting in the wardroom. Carla had her warmest coat around her shoulders. He found two blankets, wrapped one around Carla's legs and put the other around his own. They embraced and sat close together.

Carla wiped a dust mote from her eyes. "I have been trying to contact you back home for the past few weeks. When I got no response, I thought…"

"You thought what? That I didn't want to talk to you?"

She nodded. "I thought you still hadn't forgiven me."

"Forgiven you for what, for heaven's sake?"

"For the divorce."

He gave her a look of astonishment. "You felt responsible for the divorce?"

"I still do."

"Fifteen years later! That's crazy, Carla. The

divorce was never your fault. You were eleven. Your mother was simply unstable. There was nothing more to it than that. Come here."

They hugged again, holding the embrace for a few moments longer, this time. When they came apart, Carla caught a glimpse of moisture in his eyes, but it could have been a trick of the light.

"So tell me what happened, Father. Why didn't you warn me that you were leaving home?"

"I couldn't. Only a few Federation officials knew about my trip. I was sworn to secrecy."

"And Elline?"

"Elline knew, yes. When the *Vladivostok* was taken, I was captured, along with the crew. The captain saved my life. He disguised me as a crewman. The pirate chief gave the whole crew a choice: join up with him or 'walk the plank.'"

"Meaning what?"

"Meaning leave the ship through one of the airlocks."

"So, you joined the pirate gang?"

"Me, Captain Korskov, and the whole crew, with one exception."

She gave him a quizzical look.

"The Executive Officer refused."

"And?" she asked, wide-eyed.

"Captain Blackmore tossed him off the ship."

"How ghastly!"

"The rest of us joined up. We had little choice."

"Are the crew of the *Vladivostok* on board with us now?"

"No. The entire crew of the *Archangel* is on board, and Captain Korskov and one of his crewmen from the *Vladivostok*. The rest chose to remain, rather than face criminal charges in the D-System."

"What criminal charges?"

"Desertion and piracy. Capital murder, maybe."

"Won't the captain and his crewman have to face those charge?"

"Most certainly. The captain says he's willing to defend his actions."

"And you? Will you have to face those charges?"

"Perhaps. We'll burn that bridge when we come to it."

She smiled. He had always enjoyed playing with words.

"You'll need to be sure you've dotted your t's and crossed your eyes."

He laughed.

Carla said, "Do you know how the pirates gained access to the secure AD Conduit?"

"No. It seems they can create their own Gates and enter any of the Conduits whenever and wherever they like."

"That's a game changer, Father."

He nodded. "No spaceship and no space traveler is safe anymore."

She said, "Captain Blackmore never found out who you really are?"

"No, and it's to the credit of the crew that none of them told him. Now tell me why you were on board the *Archangel*. I couldn't believe it when I saw you. I had been planning my escape for some time. I was waiting for the right moment, but when I saw you I knew I couldn't wait any longer."

"I needed to retrieve one of my test subjects."

"Oscar?"

"Yes."

"Why was Oscar any more important than any other android? You can have any number of them back home."

"This one is special. The Southers stole him. It's a long story."

"We have plenty of time," said her father.

#

Lia and Oscar made themselves busy. Lia made meals for the whole crew. Oscar helped her by filling saucepans and kettles with water. Carla kept a keen eye on Lia, hoping to see signs that her hydrophobia was easing. When she saw no improvement, she ran through the coding in her mind in search of a solution.

An ancient soldering iron liberated from a maintenance locker enabled her to conduct crude running repairs on Oscar's injuries.

"I need to get you into the lab to do a better job," she said.

"Please restate the question," said Oscar.

Chapter 49

Four days after leaving the *Archangel*, the *Missie Bess* emerged into the C-System and went into orbit around Califon. Carla and her father stood at a porthole together and looked down at their shared birthplace. It looked as green and inviting as ever.

"It's beautiful," said Carla.

Both moons were at half-cycle, and looking inviting.

"Come with me," he said. "We could reclaim the old house, start again. I'm sure you'd be very happy there. It's time you settled down, found a husband."

"I'd love to, Father, but I can't," she said. "I have to take Oscar back to Earth to try and prevent a war."

"That's my girl." He kissed her forehead. "Always putting others before herself. I'll contact you as soon as I get back to Earth. Good luck with the Oscar thing."

They embraced one more time, and then he hurried away to catch a lift to the planet surface.

"Give my love to the hills behind our house,"

she said as she watched his shuttle disappear into Califon's Orbital Gate.

Overcome by a great weariness, she headed back to her cabin to sleep. As Carla climbed into her bunk, she smiled at Oscar and Lia, lying side by side on the floor of her cabin, both of them on recharge. Lia's clock preset would wake her in five hours.

#

Two hours later, Igor and two Souther crewmen slipped unseen into Carla's cabin. Carla was snoring gently in her bunk. Lia and Oscar lay side by side nearby. Igor popped the access panel and removed Oscar's powerpack. Then the men positioned themselves, one at Oscar's feet, the other at his head. At a silent signal from Igor, they lifted the AU and carried him from the cabin.

Igor led the way to a cargo bay where they placed Oscar in a rectangular box, labeled "machine parts." Igor placed Oscar's powerpack in the box and stood back while the men secured the lid with twelve screws. Then they hid it deep amid the rest of the cargo.

The three men made their way to the wardroom in search of refreshments.

"You did well," said Igor, handing out fruit bars. "That is a dangerous android and a direct threat to the Souther Federation. By securing it you have performed a great service for the Motherland."

"How is it dangerous, Comrade?" asked one of the men.

Igor smiled at the ancient appellation. These were men of the old school, men he could trust. He had chosen them carefully – and well.

"I can't tell you that, but as long as that android was in the hands of the Northers, they had a huge advantage over our Popovs in the war. When we put it into the hands of our engineers on Earth, it will be ours to exploit and the balance of power will swing our way."

"Are we at war with the Northers?" said the second man.

"No, not yet, but it is coming soon, and we will need every advantage if we are to win that war. Are you with me?"

The two men nodded.

"What will happen if the android is discovered before we can secure it on Earth?" asked the first man.

"I will ensure that nothing like that happens. But if there is any risk of it falling back into enemy hands, then it will have to be destroyed."

#

When Carla awoke, Lia was shaking her shoulder. "Wake up, Carla!"

"I'm awake, Lia. What's the matter?"

"Oscar is gone."

Carla leaped out of the bunk and threw on her

243

clothes. She had left Oscar on recharge; he should still be asleep. How could he have woken up? Where could he have gone?

She sat on the edge of the bunk and took a few deep breaths.

Oscar can't have woken by himself. That is impossible, she thought. *This is the work of the Souther engineer, Igor.*

Lia said, "Someone has taken Oscar." Carla thought she looked agitated.

They searched the ship from end to end but found no trace of Oscar. The only areas they couldn't search properly were the cargo bays, each one full to the bulkheads with a confusing jumble of contraband.

Lia looked dazed by the whole experience. "We must find him," she said.

Chapter 50

When the *Missie Bess* emerged from the AC Conduit and they could see the Earth below, there were smiles everywhere on board. Carla composed a short message to Stepan and took it to the radio operator. A line had formed. It seemed everyone on board wanted to send a message to someone on Earth. She spotted Igor in the line. He waved to her to join him, but she was too impatient to wait.

Once Captain Korskov obtained permission to land at the LAX Spaceport, the *Missie Bess* entered the Orbital Conduit and emerged through the Ground Gate. A frantic two hours of negotiations later, the crew and passengers were cleared to disembark, the Souther military forces took possession of the ship, and the stevedores went into action.

It was dark, but Carla and Lia kept Igor in their sights at all times. Lia was the one that noticed the stevedores using a crane to load a coffin-sized box into the bed of a hovertruck. And when she saw Igor climb into the cab of the truck, she gave a strange whoop and pointed. "Oscar is in a box in that hover."

Lia set off on foot after the truck.

Carla called a hovercab. "Follow that hovertruck."

"The one being chased by that mechano?"

"Yes, and step on it."

The hovertruck accelerated. The cab began to lose ground. "Can't you keep up with it?" said Carla.

"I'm sorry," said the cab driver. "These cabs have speed inhibitors. I can't even keep up with the mechano."

Carla snapped, "Her name's Lia. Explain how the truck can go faster than your cab."

"It can't. It must have its speed inhibitors removed. It's not legal."

Carla bit the inside of her cheek. She strained her eyes to keep Lia in vision, but soon lost her in the city traffic.

The cab came to a major junction. "Which way?" said the driver. Lia and the truck were gone.

"Keep going straight on," said Carla. She looked around her. They were in an unfamiliar part of the city. "Where are we?"

"Spring Street."

"Do you know the Federation Medical Research Center?"

"I know it. It's on Hill Street."

"Take me there."

It was a long shot, but it was all Carla had.

The cab turned right. Within minutes it drew up outside the Federation Medical Research building.

The cab driver said nothing until his engine cut off automatically. "Where to next, Miss?"

The building looked deserted, but as she watched, a light came on in a third-floor window. Carla considered her options. She could try to get into the building, or she could go to the lab and use her tracking system to locate Lia. A more attractive option was to go home to the apartment and wait there until Lia turned up.

She waited a few minutes more. Then she asked the cab driver to take her to the lab. He was turning the hover when she heard a shout.

She told the driver to wait and jumped out of the cab.

Lia came running from across the road. "Oscar is inside." She sounded breathless.

Breathless? AUs don't breathe!

Carla dismissed the cab. Lia led her into the hoverpark under the building. The truck was there, the crate in the bed open, empty. Carla examined it. It was labeled "machine parts."

"You think Oscar was in this box?"

"Oscar was in this box," said Lia. She sounded certain.

"You are in contact with him?"

"Yes. There are four men holding him."

"We need help," said Carla. She called Sophie. "Can you contact Benn. Tell him we need some muscle to rescue an Autonomic Unit from a group of Southers." She gave Sophie the address and broke the connection.

They found a basement entrance protected by a security keypad.

Two minutes later, Sophie returned the call. "Benn is on his way. He should be there in about ten minutes."

Carla thanked her and disconnected.

Lia said, "Oscar needs our help."

"Ten minutes. Help will be here in ten minutes."

"We can't wait," said Lia. "Oscar needs help now. Oh! he's gone. They have removed his power pack."

"Open the door," said Carla.

"I do not have the code."

"Break it," said Carla. "Smash the keypad. There's no time to waste."

Lia put a fist through the keypad, producing a mass of sparks. Carla tried the door, but it refused to open.

"Open the door, Lia."

Lia lifted a foot and drove it into the door. The door buckled. It swung open and they climbed inside.

They were in a service entrance, a staircase leading to the upper floors. Carla led the way to the third floor where a door led onto a corridor. A light shining under a door told Carla where they needed to go next.

Carla approached the door. Lia followed her. Carla listened, but heard nothing. Then someone inside the room said something that sounded like, "Turn him over."

Carla signaled to Lia. The AU put her fist through the door and they rushed inside.

Chapter 51

Oscar was lying on a table surrounded by Igor and two others. His breast panel was missing, and the three men were peering inside. They recoiled when Lia and Carla burst in.

"Get away from that AU," said Carla in her most commanding voice.

Igor stepped forward, smiling. The other two stepped back.

Lia stood between Carla and Igor, her fists still clenched. When Igor attempted to walk past her, she struck him on the side of his head. Igor fell to his knees.

He looked up at Carla. "You can't stop the inevitable."

"What does that mean?"

He got to his feet, stepping away from Lia. "I must congratulate you on your work, Miss Scott. You have built a most efficient killing machine. Our engineers back home are already working on duplicating your android's skin and my work with your assistant has shown me everything I need to duplicate your hardware module."

Carla glared at him. "Stand aside. I'm here to take possession of my android."

Igor had a disk hanging on a cord around his

neck. He pressed it and two Popovs came in through an inner door, both tall with bulging muscles. They looked like identical twins.

The tables were turned. Lia would have no chance against one of these military androids; against two, she would be torn to pieces.

Lia turned her back to Carla. "Take my powerpack."

Carla popped Lia's panel and pulled out her powerpack. Lia collapsed. While the two Souther engineers stood stupefied and the Popovs awaited orders, Carla leaped over the crouching figure of Igor and sprung Oscar's power panel open.

"Kill her! Destroy the Norther android!" Igor shouted.

The two Popovs took a step toward Carla, but before they could lay a hand on her, she slid the powerpack into place. Oscar's eyes sprang open.

The two engineers collided in their eagerness to get out through the door at the back of the room.

"Alpha Oscar, protect!" said Carla.

Oscar leaped from the table and turned to face the Popovs.

The two Popovs went into action. Following Igor's first order, they attempted to reach Carla. There was no way past the AU. Carla couldn't believe how clever Oscar was as he battled to keep two bigger, stronger opponents at bay, in spite of his twisted right knee.

Igor shouted new orders to his androids. "Leave the woman! Kill the enemy android."

As one, the Popovs reached out toward Oscar.

"Spread out. Seize him. Close in. Hold him. Knock him down."

Carla skipped out of the battle zone, giving Oscar room to swing his arms and legs. One of the Popovs went down, its legs swept out from under it. The second Popov spread its arms to enclose Oscar, but Oscar ducked and slipped out of its grasp. The first Souther android struggled to its feet and rejoined its companion. Oscar moved into the center of the room, placing the table between himself and the Popov twins. Together they moved toward Oscar. Oscar circled the table and the two Popovs followed him around the table.

"Split up!" shouted Igor, his face turning an interesting shade of scarlet.

One of the Popovs turned and circled the table the other way. But when they reached Oscar and attempted to grab him from two sides, he sprang up onto the table. He kicked one of the Popovs full in the face before jumping down on the opposite side and upending the table. Both Popovs went down, but they got up again immediately, one of them smashing the table with its arm, splitting it in two. One of the Popovs picked up a knife from a work surface and both of them advanced toward Oscar again. Oscar stood his ground. The android with the knife drove the blade into Oscar's midriff. Oscar roared. Picking up a chair, he swung it, catching his attacker a shattering blow that sent it flying to the far corner of the room, where it lay still.

The remaining android wrapped an arm around Oscar's neck. Oscar grappled with it. His missing breast panel gave the Popov a point of attack, but every time it tried to reach around to put a hand inside his chest, Oscar ducked or twisted out of its grasp. Finally, he broke free and delivered a crushing blow as he spun away. The Popov pounced again. Anticipating the move, Oscar maneuvered the Popov into an arm hold and broke its arm at the elbow. Carla winced. Then Oscar grabbed the Popov's left knee and finished the job. The Popov collapsed to the floor, writhing around in an attempt to stand and fight.

With a red glint in his one good eye, Oscar turned on Igor.

"Keep him away from me!" screamed Igor.

He made a dash for the door, but Oscar was too fast. He caught the engineer with a blow to the chest that knocked him to the floor. Reaching down, Oscar grabbed the engineer by an ankle with his left hand, and upended him, lifting the tall engineer clear off the ground.

Carla feared for what Oscar might do next. She stepped into Oscar's line of sight. "Put him down, Oscar."

Ignoring Carla's command, Oscar wrapped the other hand around Igor's right ankle, crushing it. Igor screamed.

"Alpha Oscar, who am I?"

"You are Carla Scott," said Oscar, lifting Igor higher. Igor continued screaming.

"I am Carla Scott and I'm ordering you to release that man, code one seven one five two three."

Oscar tossed Igor through the window. The glass shattered, setting off the building's alarms. Igor fell three floors, to his death.

Igor had not exaggerated. Oscar had become a killing machine. Carla knew he would have to be destroyed. She ordered Oscar to stand still. Oscar placed his arms by his sides.

She went around behind him, but before she could access his power panel, he twisted his torso and seized her arm. "I need to live," he said.

"Alpha Oscar, you know who I am."

"You are Carla Scott."

"Yes, I am Carla Scott and I'm ordering you to sleep. Code one five one seven—"

"I need to live," said Oscar.

"Let go of my arm, Alpha Oscar, and go to sleep. Code one five one seven two three."

Oscar said nothing. Looking strangely content, he let go of Carla's arm. He picked up his chest panel from the workbench and fixed it in place. Then he strode to the door.

She watched in awe as Oscar disobeyed her, something that she'd thought impossible. Technically, when he threw Igor through the window, he had obeyed her order to put the man down, but this was undisputable insubordination; Oscar had defied her and refused a direct order.

Her backdoor access had never failed before; it

was foolproof, or so she thought. Her mind began to tackle the puzzle.

"Alpha Oscar 113, where are you going?" she said.

Oscar gave no answer – another near impossibility. He opened the door and stepped outside.

"Alpha Oscar! Come back," she called after him.

Oscar was gone.

Chapter 52

Carla carried Lia down the stairs as the alarms continued to scream. The glass of the front door lay in smithereens where Oscar had smashed his way out of the building. Carla carried Lia out and ducked away from the building. Benn and his crew arrived just in time to whisk them away moments before the first police hovers arrived.

Back in her apartment, Carla found a spare powerpack for Lia and started her programs. She plugged in her soldering iron.

"What happened? Where is Oscar?" said Lia as soon as she was awake.

"Oscar fought the two enemy androids and won. I don't know where he is."

Lia closed her eyes. "Oscar is walking north. He has pain in his body."

"One of the Popovs stabbed him. Tell him to come here. I will repair his damage."

A few moments passed as Carla began to repair Lia's two bullet wounds. Then Lia looked at Carla. "Oscar will not come here. He says you will end him."

"Where is he going?"

"North."

Carla said nothing.

"Will you end Oscar?"

"I must end him. Oscar is out of control. He killed a man, and he may have killed another man on the freighter."

When Carla had finished the repair work, Lia went into the kitchen without another word. Carla assumed she was preparing some food, but, when she heard no sounds from the kitchen, she went to investigate. Lia was standing in the middle of the room, staring at a blank wall.

"Where is he now?" said Carla.

"I cannot reach Oscar."

"Is he sleeping?"

"No, he has switched off his telecommunications module."

Carla knew of no way that an AU could disable any of its own modules. Another puzzle to solve! In her mind she set about looking for the solution.

Lia began to prepare a meal, but once again balked at the faucet. Carla filled a saucepan and a kettle for her. While Lia made the meal, Carla checked her X-Vid. She had 23 missed calls. Twelve were from Fritz Franck, two from Major Grant. Most of the rest were from Stepan. She turned on the TV. As soon as news of the loss of the second freighter reached the trade talks on Califon, the negotiations had broken down again. She watched a rerun of a speech by the premier of the Souther Bloc where he declared that the ceasefire had failed. The two superpowers were now irrevocably at war.

War!

The Southers held both Ground Gates on Earth, the one in Eastern Europe and the one at Los Angeles International Spaceport. They had thousands of troops and many times more Popovs on Norther Federation soil already and a fleet of troop transports waiting in orbit. Control of the two Gates meant they could land their troops from their orbiting ships immediately and move as many as they wished from the D-System any time they wished. The Northers, on the other hand, were limited to what troops they had on Earth, with no possibility of adding reinforcements from any of the other colonies. The only other supply of Norther troops was on Lunar1, 48 hours away by conventional engines.

The battle for LAX had begun. Its outcome would decide the war, and which of the superpowers would control the colonies in the centuries to come.

#

Carla hurried to the hospital, where she found Sophie keeping vigil beside Cassidy's bed. Cassidy was no better than he had been.

"Has he opened his eyes or spoken while I was away?" asked Carla.

Sophie's eyes were red and swollen. "No. I'm

afraid the doctors will turn off his respirator, soon."

Carla checked the machines for brain activity. "They won't do that. He's still with us."

She gave Sophie a parting hug and headed to Feynman Tech in a cab.

The professor was pleased to see her, although the news from the battleground was etched in worry lines on his face.

"Tell me you have something to help end this madness," he said.

"I may have, Professor." She grabbed a pen and drew a series of quick sketches on the professor's pad.

"Cassidy and I completed the pain element. Problems arose when we tried to program the responses."

"You spoke of a Fear module."

"Fear, yes. We had some successes, but one of our test subjects developed an extreme level of anger when subjected to pain. There was evidence that they were warning each other what to expect in the lab, and we saw lots of different reactions, from apprehension through terror. The terror was a response to anticipated pain rather than actual pain experienced."

"Interesting."

"Others became obdurate. One – my personal domestic – developed a phobia."

"That's fascinating," said the professor. "Is there anything useful in all that?"

"There may be. I have converted the module entirely to software, which means I could release it to every AU soldier on Earth."

"What effect would it have?"

"Statistically, I would expect the AUs to be more circumspect, more careful in the battlefield. Any that suffer an injury would take evasive action in order to avoid further injury."

"That should help."

"I think so, but we must anticipate that a small number may react with extreme anger. They could be a danger to their fellow Units. We have one test subject who is now a killer. He has killed one man for certain and possibly one more."

"Where is this Unit now?"

Carla shook her head. "I don't know. The last I heard he was heading north."

"Toward the Spaceport."

"Yes."

"So, what are you planning to do, Carla?"

"I'm not sure. I could take a chance and release what I have to all the Norther Units, but the risks are enormous. It could turn them all into craven cowards."

"Or psychopathic killers."

Chapter 53

Carla switched on the TV in her apartment. Xeno-Fox were showing reruns of an ancient show called *I Love Lucy*. The battle for the Spaceport was featured on every news channel. It made for compulsive viewing, with cameras strategically placed all around the battleground. The two armies were of similar sizes. The Southers were besieged behind barricades within the Spaceport, holding their positions with relative ease. The Northers' forward base was in the airport building.

Lia sat on the couch beside Carla, hands clasped in her lap.

The commentary was a grim monotony. *The Southers have every advantage. They hold the all-important Spaceport, and that has been built to survive an earthquake. If the Northers want to recapture the Spaceport, they will have to traverse the runways, where there is no cover, only wide-open ground and dozens of huge craters. It will take something extraordinary for our forces to win this battle. The Southers can sit tight. The Northers have no fear...*

Carla nodded. She thought, *Apart from one AU, the Northers have no fear.*

"Can you see the screen there, Lia?" Carla asked.

There was no response.

"Lia?"

Lia turned her head to face Carla. "Oscar is close to the fighting."

"You are in contact with him?"

"He has pain in his body."

"That knife that Popov stuck in his stomach."

Our guys are going in. The commentator's voice trembled with excitement. Carla and Lia watched as wave after wave of Norther AUs attacked the defenses and were cut down by lethal fire from the Souther blasters. With ever-decreasing spirits she saw her Autonomic Units charge headlong into the fray with no regard for their own safety. She was reminded of the famous charge of the Light Brigade, the futile assaults across no man's land during the first great war of the twentieth century and the battle for Mare Vaporium of the Second Lunar War. Those were men of flesh and blood that died, but the comparison was striking. It seemed wars were fought today as they had always been fought: Plutocrats throwing vast armies of cannon fodder at one another.

Lia stood up suddenly and offered to make tea.

"Thank you, Lia," said Carla. "There's water in the kettle."

An explosion on the battlefield drew Carla's attention to the screen. Lia turned back to watch. Parts of the airport building were on fire, flames reaching high into the clouds. Light from the fire showed AUs moving away from the conflagration, taking up new positions.

Lia leaped in the air. "There is Oscar!"

Carla peered at the screen. All she could see was a jumble of figures in silhouette, AUs moving about, taking up defensive positions. "Where is he?"

"There!" Lia pointed. "Oscar has a blaster."

Carla picked out a crouching, limping figure leading an assault. It could have been Oscar, but it was impossible to be sure.

The TV commentator's voice rose in intensity. *The Northers are regrouping. They are advancing again. If this was a test of courage, we would win, hands down. But the Southers are well dug-in and they have superior firepower.*

The battle intensified. The Northers gained some ground and stormed a building on the Southers' left flank. Then a second explosion ripped through the advancing troops.

"Oh!" said Lia.

"What happened?"

"I do not know. Oscar fell. I lost contact with him."

Flashes of blaster fire from the Spaceport lit up the scene. There was very little return fire from the airport building or the remnants of the

Norther attack force, scattered among the cratered runways.

The TV commentator's voice dropped. *That last explosion has decimated our forces. They need to withdraw. They need covering fire. Where's the covering fire?* He sounded despairing. *Someone needs to take charge. They should be using artillery or air power. This is a battle that we must not lose, that we cannot lose. As long as the Southers have the Spaceport, they can rule the galaxy.*

"Oscar!" said Lia.

Carla looked up at her. "You've spoken to him again? He is alive?"

"Yes, Oscar is alive. He has more pain on his body."

"Sit here," said Carla. "I'll make the tea. We're in for a long night."

#

The battle continued to rage through the night. The Northers made small gains only to be driven back again.

This is hopeless, said the commentator. *The two armies are too evenly matched, although if truth be told, the Souther androids probably have the edge. They are smarter that the Northers. If they weren't so concerned about holding the Spaceport, they could easily come across and overrun the Northers.*

Carla put Lia on recharge for an hour. As the AU slept, she prepared Lia's software module for transmission.

When she woke Lia, she asked, "Are you still in contact with Oscar?"

"Yes, Oscar is damaged."

That was a worry, but Carla had to go ahead with her plan. "I have prepared your new module for transmission. I want you to send it to Oscar."

Within minutes Lia confirmed that Oscar now had a copy of her software module.

"That's good," said Carla. "Ask him to confirm that it has installed."

"Oscar has not installed the module."

Carla ground her teeth. Oscar had interfered with the auto-install. He was not just disobedient, he was obstinate, impossible to deal with, pigheaded, unreasonable, insubordinate, irritating and smart. Just like any man.

"Now transmit the software to all the other military Units."

After a pause, Lia said, "Oscar says no."

"What do you mean?"

"Oscar has told me not to transmit to the other AUs."

"Tell him the order is from me."

Another pause. Then, "Oscar says no."

Carla took a deep breath. *What an infuriating android!*

"Tell him the module will help the Northers to win the war. Tell him they need to feel pain to make them smarter than the Popovs."

There was a long pause. Then Lia said, "Oscar says I may comply."

Chapter 54

As Carla watched, she could see the software installation running through the Autonomic Units like ripples on the surface of a pond. First, whenever an AU was injured, he took evasive action. Then, as warnings passed through from injured Units to the others, they all began to take precautions. AUs were seen sheltering in rain-filled shell holes, advancing in small stages from crater to crater, firing as they went. Then injured Units started removing themselves from the conflict, allowing fresh Units to take their places. Those too badly injured to move were carried to safety by their comrades. The changes became more and more noticeable, and the cumulative effect was of an army of intelligent soldiers, no longer hell-bent on destruction, but working together toward their common goal.

The Norther advance ground to a halt with hundreds of soldiers holed up in craters while others returned to base to recharge. The Southers held their positions in the Spaceport. And everything went quiet. Both armies had fought themselves to exhaustion. They were in stalemate.

At about 3 a.m. a force of Southers emerged from their stronghold, advanced across the runways, and stormed the airport building. They encountered very little resistance. Carla watched in horror as each section of the building fell in turn, sending the Northers – AUs and flesh and blood officers – scrambling away in retreat. The screen went blank and was replaced by a man in a studio.

It appears our top brass has decided to smoke the Southers out by cutting off their power. Without electricity they had no way of recharging the Popovs' powerpacks. The result, as you saw, was not what was hoped for. The Southers took the only action they could, and counterattacked. They now have control of every part of the LAX complex, including all the generators and all the biofuel they need to run them.

Carla was exhausted. She lay down on her bed, intending to grab a few minutes rest, and fell into a deep sleep.

#

When Carla awoke, she heard voices in the kitchen. She checked her clock. She'd been asleep for three hours. A glimmer of light in the sky told her that dawn was approaching. She went to investigate, and found Lia in the kitchen in conversation with Oscar.

Oscar was in a bad state. He'd lost his left arm below the elbow, his right leg was bent at an unnatural angle, and there were blaster burns all over his body.

"Oscar, you're injured," said Carla. "Sit down and I'll see what I can do to repair the damage."

Oscar turned his one good eye toward Carla. "You will end me."

"No, Oscar, I want to help you. Sit down."

Lia said, "Oscar will not sit. He does not wish to be repaired."

"Why not?"

"You will end Oscar. You said you must end him."

Carla crossed her arms. Oscar was not wrong. Nothing had changed. She had a duty to terminate him as soon as the opportunity presented itself.

"Why did you come back?" she asked him.

Oscar's one eye was fixed on her. He made no reply.

Lia said, "Oscar returned for me."

"He came back for you?" Carla couldn't believe her ears.

"Yes. He has asked me to go with him."

Carla's mind was racing, now. Could her Pain-Fear module have created something else, some form of intimate connection between two Autonomic Units? Could the sharing of feelings of pain and fear develop into something deeper? Something like affection? Or love? She shook her head. There was nothing in the coding to suggest the possibility of anything like that. And yet the evidence was standing in front of her.

"Where will you go?" she said.

Oscar replied, "Somewhere in the Six Systems."

"We will find somewhere," said Lia, moving closer to Oscar. Her hand brushed against his one remaining hand, and he grasped it.

We! They are a couple.

"Let me repair you," said Carla. "You wouldn't last long out there with only one arm."

Oscar looked away, and the two AUs had a silent conversation. Then Lia said, "Oscar will allow this."

"Lia must remain with me," said Oscar. His meaning was clear.

Carla took Oscar and Lia to the lab in a hovercab. At Xenodyne Automation, the night watchman gave them a strange look, but he let them pass. Lia powered Oscar down and watched closely while Carla repaired his arm, replaced his broken camera and patched up the various cuts in his skin. She found a replacement leg in Cassidy's corner of the workshop. When she'd finished, she topped up Oscar's hydraulic fluid, fitted a new breast panel, and put him on recharge.

While Oscar slept, Carla spoke with Lia.

"You are fond of Oscar, I think."

Lia said nothing. Carla needed to formulate a question.

"Are you friends with Oscar?"

"Yes," said Lia. "I am safe when he is near."

"You are safe here, with me," said Carla.

Lia said nothing.

"Is Oscar friends with you?"

"Oscar and I are friends," said Lia. "We will go away together."

"Where will you go?"

Lia stared at nothing over Carla's shoulder. "Oscar says we will go to the C-System. We have both seen Califon from orbit."

"Califon is beautiful," said Carla.

Lia said, "Yes, Califon is beautiful."

#

Lia woke Oscar. He got to his feet, looked around the lab and flexed his new arm.

"How do you feel, Oscar?" said Carla.

"My sight is restored."

"And how's your arm and your leg?"

"My arm is restored. My leg is restored." He turned to Lia. "We can go now."

"I need to recharge," said Lia.

Carla closed up the lab and took Lia and Oscar back to the apartment. As soon as they arrived, she put Lia on recharge. Oscar remained standing close to Lia, keeping his distance from Carla. While Carla waited for the coffee to percolate, she put on some alternative jazz music on a low volume.

"Nick Nelton," said Oscar, "the greatest jazz pianist of his generation."

The comment surprised Carla. She had no idea where Oscar could have picked up an appreciation for music. Probably something Cassidy did.

She took her coffee to the table and looked at the AU. He was carrying a lot of scars, but he was still a fine figure of an android, a perfect match for her Lia. But would they make it to Califon together? And if they made it to their paradise, would they survive there? Oscar was still a lethal weapon, a danger to humanity, a killing machine beyond her control. Could she allow him to leave? Did she have the power to prevent it?

Oscar broke through her thoughts with a surprising statement, "The Souther engineer gave me a message for you."

"Who? Igor, the one you killed?"

"I did not kill Igor," said Oscar. "I broke his leg."

"Yes, and then you threw him out of a window on the third floor."

"I did not kill him."

Carla understood the fine distinction Oscar was making. He didn't kill Igor. It was the impact with the ground that killed him.

"What was the message?"

"He said you were the greatest android engineer in the Six Systems."

"Very flattering," said Carla.

Chapter 55

Carla said, "Remember when we were on that freighter in the CD Conduit? You communicated with the Popovs."

Oscar replied, "I asked them to help us."

"Yes, and they helped us when we tried to recover the ship."

"Igor was on the bridge with the pirate captain."

"Can you still communicate with the Popovs?"

"Yes."

Carla swallowed a lump in her throat. "Could you transmit Lia's new software module to the Popovs in the Spaceport?"

Oscar tilted his head and looked at her. "Why would you wish that?"

"Just tell me if you can do it."

"I can, but the software will not be compatible with the enemy android systems."

"Oscar, the Souther android systems are completely compatible with yours. The technology has been stolen from my lab over many years and given to their engineers."

Oscar took a few moments to absorb this information. "If that was true the Popovs in Igor's lab would have beaten me."

Carla shook her head. "Their hardware is different. They are slower, heavier, and they don't have skin like yours."

He paused again. "Tell me how the enemy obtained your technology."

"I don't know the answer to that question, Oscar. Somebody has been passing my secrets to the enemy over many years."

"Cassidy," said Oscar. It wasn't a question. Logic suggested Cassidy was the prime suspect, but there were others.

"No, I don't think so."

"Who?" said Oscar. "Tell me who and I will kill him."

Carla laughed nervously. "No need for that. I will fix the problem. Now, I'd like you to transmit Lia's new Fear module to the Popovs at the Spaceport."

Oscar hesitated.

"Do it. Now," she commanded.

Oscar strode into the kitchen where Lia was lying. He disconnected her from the recharger, waking her. Lia sat up. Oscar held out his new hand and helped her to her feet.

She said, "It is time I started preparing a meal for Carla."

Oscar took her elbow and steered her into the lounge.

"Tell Lia," he said to Carla.

Carla said, "I have asked Oscar to transmit the new module to the enemy Popovs."

"Why would you do that?" said Lia.

"The software is compatible with the Popovs' system—"

"Carla Scott's systems have been stolen by the enemy," said Oscar.

"That's right," said Carla. "Someone has been passing my work to the Southers for many years. The point is that your new module is compatible with their systems."

"You want Oscar to send them my new module?"

"Yes."

"Please explain."

"It's too complicated to explain," said Carla. "Both of you need to trust me when I say it is the right thing to do."

Oscar said, "It would be good to give the Southers pain."

"You will do it?" said Carla.

"I will do it if Lia says it is okay," said Oscar.

Lia pondered for a minute. Then she said, "I trust Carla. Do it."

Five minutes later, Oscar had transmitted Lia's new Fear module to one of the Popovs with instructions to distribute it to them all.

Carla switched on the TV.

The coverage was from cameras mounted in helihovers, the view obscured by a fog rolling in from the ocean.

All is quiet down there, said a familiar voice. *The Souther androids now have possession of the whole of LAX Airport and Spaceport. Our guys are building their numbers, but I think we can be sure the Southers are bringing in reinforcements from their troopships in orbit above us. Meanwhile, the people of LA are heading out.* The camera panned across to the Interstate 5 Highway where a million hovers were stacked in a 500-mile traffic jam. *Who can blame them? If I wasn't contractually obliged to ride this helihover, I'd be down there with my wife and family heading for the hills.*

Lia and Oscar sat beside Carla on the couch.

A cloud of dust rose from the vicinity of the Spaceport.

Did you see that? The commentator's voice rose with excitement. *A ship has just entered the Ground Gate. And I don't think it was carrying a load of holidaymakers heading to Disneyland. You can bet that was a troop transport landing yet more murdering Popovs. It must be clear to everyone now that the Southers intend to seize control of the Federation and the entire Six Systems of the galaxy. And they don't care who gets killed in the process.*

What have we heard from the premier of the Souther Bloc in recent days? Nothing. And what has our president been doing? Your guess is as good as mine. The good people of California, and not just Los Angeles, should be warned: When this behemoth starts to move, thousands will die. Nevada will be next, followed by Oregon and

Washington after that. I can see waves of Popovs sweeping across this fair land of ours from west to east. Millions will die.

He put a finger to his earpiece. *Hold on, there's a message coming through from my producer in the studio. Okay, folks, maybe I was exaggerating, just a bit, but I'll leave it to you to make up your own minds. Are we screwed or are we totally screwed?*

The picture switched back to a news anchor in the studio. He smiled sheepishly. *That was Chuck Chandler, ever the optimist. The situation in Los Angeles Air- and Spaceport is quite... er, uncertain... but there's no need for panic. The president is consulting with the Secretary of State. We expect a statement from him shortly. Meanwhile, here's some music...* A field full of daffodils filled the screen, accompanied by Beethoven's pastoral symphony.

Carla crossed her legs. She flicked to Xeno-Fox. The ten thousandth rerun of *Friends* had just started. Lia and Oscar both turned to look at her. She found another news channel.

...from the president. Now we're switching over to the White House where our correspondent Marge Bobbard is standing by. Marge?

Thank you, Bill. We are expecting a statement from the president in the next few moments. Stay with us. The Secretary of State has been in consultation with the president for hours, and we have seen several generals come and go during the morning, notably General Matthewson, the commander of the Western Army. I think we can anticipate a strong condemnation from the White House of the Southers' aggressive actions on our shores.

The picture switched back to the anchor in California. *Yes, Marge, but can we expect anything more than words? What this situation needs is direct action, I think you must agree…*

Carla switched back to Xeno-Fox in time to see Joey make an ass of himself in *Friends*. She switched back.

The screen was split now, showing the anchor on the left and Marge Bobbard on the right. Marge touched her earpiece. *We are ready for the president now.*

Chapter 56

The cameras switched to the White House where the president sat at his desk.

Good morning my fellow Northers, he began. *As you are all aware, the Souther Bloc has invaded our western shores, bringing death and destruction to the people of Southern California. The seizure of our Spaceport and Ground Gate at Los Angeles is a blatant act of war. It will not stand.* He paused. *The enemy continues to flood our land with android soldiers from their fleet in orbit. I have ordered our Space Corps to send a detachment of fighters to disperse that hostile fleet, and they are already inbound from Lunar1. Meanwhile, I have ordered our generals to take every necessary step on the ground to eject the enemy from Los Angeles. These actions by the Southers have placed the Federation at serious risk. It is to be regretted that our joint enterprise of one hundred and twenty years has been placed in absolute jeopardy by these reckless actions. But we will stand against this enemy and we will prevail. Long live the Norther Federation.*

The first journalist asked what specific action

the army planned to take to recover LAX. The president declined to answer, citing national security. Another journalist asked why the Norther androids seemed inferior to their counterparts, the Souther Popovs. The president left the room, leaving the Secretary of State to answer that question.

We have every faith in our armed services. As I'm sure you are all aware, our military is working with Xenodyne Automation to constantly upgrade and improve the performance of our wonderful Autonomic Units. These Souther Units are heavier and stronger, but ours are faster and smarter. It may take a while, but we will triumph in the end.

Carla switched back to the original news station in time to see the Secretary of State winding up the session. The picture switched back to the view from the helihover over LAX.

Something is happening down there.

A missile shot past the helihover and exploded on a runway. The helihover veered away from the scene, the camera catching the volley of rockets that followed.

The Northers are fighting back! shouted the commentator.

Carla glanced at Oscar and Lia sitting on the couch; they were holding hands like a couple at the movies.

The helihover took up a position a mile from the Spaceport and the camera zoomed in on the action. Missiles struck the Spaceport. Carla blinked. She couldn't believe what happened next. A group of Popovs emerged. Throwing away their blasters, they raised their hands in the air, first three or four, then twenty. The camera panned beyond the Spaceport perimeter to the west, where Popovs were running, fifty, two hundred, a thousand, all fleeing for their lives through the sea mist.

Lia clapped her hands. Oscar made a small sound that Carla couldn't identify or categorize.

The Southers are giving up! screamed the commentator. *I don't believe this. It must be a trick.*

But Carla knew it wasn't. Fear without pain induced abject terror.

#

The Northers quickly took possession of the Spaceport and the Souther generals conceded defeat. Two hundred Souther soldiers were rounded up and placed in custody. Thousands of Popovs had their powerpacks removed and were unceremoniously decommissioned.

A red-faced president appeared on TV again, full of praise for the brave Norther androids. He announced that the hero of the engagement, General Matthewson, was to be given a medal. In a rare demonstration of magnanimity, he offered to resume the trade talks – on Earth, this time –

subject to an unconditional concession by the Southers of all forestry rights on Pondieskaya, the jewel of the D-System. The Norther Federation Food Commissioner would be recalled to Earth and asked to lead the negotiations.

Carla's heart leaped in her chest when she heard that. Her father would be home soon. She had so much catching up to do.

Her X-Vid buzzed. It was Fritz Franck.

"I hope you're watching the performance of your military Units on TV," said her boss.

"What do you want, Fritz?" she snapped.

"Report to my office at ten a.m. tomorrow." He cut the call before she could object.

She handed the TV remote to Lia and went to have a shower.

Chapter 57

Water jets caressed Carla's tired body from every angle. She sang. She was barely aware that she was singing. Her work on the Fear module had born fruit beyond her wildest imaginings. It was still a blunt instrument, but with experimentation she was confident it could be refined. Perhaps she could use it to develop all sorts of emotions in her AUs. Lia and Oscar had already shown what could be possible.

She reached for the shampoo, and a hand grabbed her wrist. Sweeping the water from her eyes, she was confronted by Oscar, a red glint in his eyes.

"Let go of me!"

Gripping her wrist, he stepped into the shower with her.

"Oscar, what are you doing?" The situation would have been comical if he wasn't hurting her. And she knew she had more to worry about than a sore wrist. She was sharing a shower with a proven killer.

"Oscar, who am I?" she said.

"You are Carla Scott."

"I am Carla Scott and I'm ordering you to release me. Code one five—"

He grabbed her by the throat, pushing her under the overhead showerhead.

"Alpha Oscar, take your hand from my throat," she croaked.

Oscar lifted her off her feet, cutting off her airflow. She had seconds left to live.

"You will not end me," he said.

And then she was lying in the shower tray beside an inert Autonomic Unit. She looked up. Lia was standing holding Oscar's powerpack, backing away from the flowing water with a wild look in her eyes.

Carla put a hand to her throat. She coughed. "Thank you, Lia." Her voice was barely audible.

Lia dropped the powerpack and ran from the bathroom. Carla turned off the water. Then she opened Oscar's breast panel and pulled out his four main modules, Perception, Orientation, Compliance and Cognition. Without those, Oscar was nothing but a bundle of metal glass and polymers.

She wrapped a towel around her and went to speak with Lia.

She found Lia sitting on the couch shivering, frantically brushing water from her clothes. Carla recognized a severe phobic panic attack. She put Lia to sleep. Then she removed Lia's wet clothes, dried her hair and body, and dressed her in a dry outfit from the wardrobe.

When Carla woke her again, Lia was perfectly calm. She said, "You ended Oscar?"

"Yes, I'm sorry."

"Oscar was bad."

"No, Lia, my module did that to him. It was my fault."

"But you ended him."

"I had to end him."

"He would have ended you," said Lia.

"Yes. Why did you stop him?"

"He would have ended you, Carla Scott."

That bland statement said it all, and yet it told Carla nothing. What had inspired Lia to save Carla's life? Was it duty, loyalty, or something else? Was the code in her Compliance module enough to explain her actions, or was there something deeper? Something like empathy or a compulsion to help someone in trouble, perhaps? Or a feeling of friendship? Carla searched Lia's eyes for a spark of humanity but found nothing.

"I wanted..."

"I'm sorry, Lia."

Later, while Lia was preparing a meal, Carla went into the lounge and switched on the TV. Xeno-Fox were running a season of Charlie Chaplin's silent movies. She settled down to watch *The Gold Rush*.

She dozed off.

She was woken by a strange sound coming from the kitchen and went to investigate.

Lia lay on the floor, her knees pulled up to her

chest, making a strange low keening sound.

Carla helped her to her feet and held her.

Lia wrapped her arms around Carla. "Oscar asked me to go to Califon. I wanted to go with him."

"I know. I'm really sorry, Lia."

Lia the android was crying.

Chapter 58

The next morning, while Carla slept, Lia retrieved Oscar's four modules. She placed them in a gym bag and hid the bag in a kitchen cabinet.

"How are feeling this morning, Lia?" asked Carla after her shower.

"Breakfast will be ready in three minutes," said Lia, brightly.

Carla was relieved to see no sign of Lia's distress of the night before.

She rang Stepan.

"Where have you been?" he said. "I've been trying to reach you."

"Why?"

"No special reason. I was worried about you."

"I need your help," she said.

"Just tell me what you need."

"I have to go to work. I have been away from the lab for a couple of weeks and I will have to explain why. I'm expecting a stormy meeting."

"Okay, how can I help?"

"I'd like you to come with me, to give me moral support."

"I can do that. I'll meet you there. What time?"

#

Carla and Stepan made their way up the stairs to Fritz Franck's office. His secretary showed them inside, without a word.

Dr. Franck was seated behind his desk, smoking a cigar. Major Grant, the security chief, was sitting facing him.

"Who's this?" said Franck.

"This is Stepan. He's here to protect my interests," said Carla.

"Are you her lawyer?" said Grant.

"I'm her boyfriend," Stepan replied.

He wasn't, but she let that go.

Franck stood up. "This is most irregular." He glared at Grant. "How did this person get past security?"

Grant got to his feet. Now they were all standing. "I must ask you to leave the building." He took a step toward Stepan.

Carla held up a hand to stop him. "If Stepan leaves, then I leave."

Grant turned to Franck for guidance and Franck waved his cigar. "Very well, take a seat at the table. And don't speak unless you're spoken to."

Stepan sat at the table and Carla moved to do the same.

"Not you, Ms. Scott," Franck growled. "You sit here." He pointed to the chair in the center of the room, to the right of Grant's.

Carla took that chair. She crossed her arms and her legs.

Franck pressed his intercom. "Lydda, please let Ricarda Petrik know that Carla Scott is in my office. She will want to be present for this interview. And find another chair for her."

A few moments later, Lynda came in with a chair which she placed to Carla's right. "Ms. Petrik is on her way," she said.

Carla prepared herself to meet the wife of a serial fraudster. She needed to put the TV news article about Petrik's husband out of her mind.

"Does *he* have to be here?" said Carla, nodding her head toward Major Grant.

"I will decide who is and is not at this meeting," said Franck. "We will all just wait until Ricarda Petrik gets here."

It wasn't long before the CFO arrived, but by that time Franck's office stank of tobacco. A thin veil of smoke hung in the air.

"Put that disgusting thing out and open a window," said Petrik.

Franck stubbed out his cigar. Lynda shot across the office and opened the window.

Petrik nodded a greeting to Carla as she sat down. Carla responded with a wide-eyed look that told the CFO what she was thinking.

Lynda left the room, and Franck cleared his throat. "I've called this meeting to discuss Carla Scott's work performance. Over the past two weeks, she has been largely absent from her laboratory—"

Petrik cut across him. "I don't think so. I am

here to congratulate Ms. Scott and her assistant on the spectacular success of their latest development work."

Franck raised his voice to protest. "I have had to fend off persistent demands from our military generals for performance updates on work in progress that has fallen behind agreed schedules."

Petrik turned to Carla. "How is Cassidy, by the way?"

"He is still recovering, as far as I know. I hope to visit him later today."

"I'm told he fell from a roof?"

"He was abducted by a team of Souther engineers and forced to work with them. He fell while trying to escape."

Petrik shook her head. "Send him my best wishes."

"I will, thank you, Ma'am."

Franck continued, "Carla's recent actions have placed all our military contracts in jeopardy. Deadlines have to be met. You know how important it is that we meet our military deadlines." He sounded like a petulant child.

Petrik gave Franck an icy stare. "To my certain knowledge, Xenodyne Automation is the only enterprise anywhere in the Norther territories manufacturing Autonomic Units. Where else can the military get their androids? And it may have slipped your notice, but our military have been engaged in a war this past week. I think we can conclude that military priorities have shifted."

Franck's gaze dropped to his desk.

Petrik continued, "We are not here to discuss your problems, Dr. Franck. Let us hear what Ms. Scott has to say before we rush to judgment."

Carla took a deep breath. "Thank you, Ms. Petrik. I think you appreciate the role that Cassidy's groundbreaking new module had in the battle for LAX."

Grant harrumphed.

Franck peered into his ashtray as if he might recover his crushed cigar. "If you are referring to the way our androids hid in shell holes, then I think we all saw how that worked."

Carla said, "That was what kept them alive. And that was one of the factors that led to their eventual success and the recapture of the Spaceport."

Grant harrumphed again.

"Bless you," said Carla.

Grant pointed a bony finger in her direction. "Your idea of what makes a good soldier is not what we are here to discuss."

"No, indeed," said Petrik. "I would like to hear Ms. Scott's explanation for the cowardice of the enemy androids. I have never witnessed such a complete collapse of morale in battle and I believe she did something that caused it. Am I right?"

"That's ridiculous," said Grant.

Carla began her explanation of what happened. "First, we succeeded in building a Pain-Fear module that enabled the AUs to react to injury.

Wireless communication between the Units, even in the lab, allowed them to pass on warnings to each other. Once I had distributed this module to the AUs on the battlefield, they began to act sensibly, protecting themselves and each other from harm."

"That is all very encouraging," said Petrik.

"Thank you," said Carla. "Then we discovered that the Fear module on its own, without the pain element, induces extreme terror."

"And that is what you gave to the Popovs?"

"Yes."

"With spectacular results." Petrik beamed at her.

"Hold on a minute," said Franck. "You installed this new module in our AUs through telecommunications links, right?"

"That's correct," said Carla.

"How did you install the Fear module in the enemy androids?"

"By the same method."

"That's preposterous." Grant snorted.

"You expect us to believe that you could communicate across the airwaves with the enemy forces?" said Franck.

"You can believe what you wish," said Carla.

A moment of silence followed. Carla felt obliged to explain, given the puzzled look on Petrik's face. "Following the first battle for the Spaceport, the military gave me an enemy Popov to examine..."

"Why wasn't I told about that?" said Grant.

"A dead one, I hope," said Petrik.

"It had its powerpack removed, yes," said Carla. "That was all I needed to allow me to communicate with the Popovs."

"All of them?" said Grant.

"Of course. They are all the same."

Petrik stood up. "I, for one, am happy with the outcome of your work. Well done, and well done to your assistant, also. I hope he makes a full recovery."

Franck said, "Carla continued to work on the PREM project, despite the fact that it had been cancelled on your express order."

"I think we can overlook that, don't you?" said Petrik.

"Her other projects were abandoned for at least three weeks. The generals—"

"I'm sure the generals will be delighted when they receive my report. Carla Scott has saved the Spaceport, the A-System, and the Federation single-handed." Petrik looked at her watch.

"There is one other matter that I'd like to discuss, before you go," said Carla.

Chapter 59

Ricarda Petrik returned to her seat.

"As I said, I had an opportunity to examine the inner workings of a Popov, and what I discovered was quite shocking." Carla paused.

"Are you going to tell us?" said Grant.

"There are differences between the Popovs and the AUs, but I was surprised to discover that the Popovs' four main modules are exactly the same as our AUs: Perception, Orientation, Cognition and Compliance."

"Is that such a surprise?" said Grant.

"Perhaps not, but when I looked at the code in the four modules, I found something really disturbing." She paused again. "Significant pieces of the code are mine."

"You mean the Souther code resembles yours," said Grant.

Carla shook her head. "I mean the Popovs are using code that I wrote three years ago, line by line, word for word, character by character."

Grant leaned so far forward, he nearly fell out of his chair. "Are you saying your code was stolen and sold to the enemy?"

"Yes, without question."

Petrik blanched.

Grant said, "We have a mole!"

Franck balled his hands into fists. "Do you know who's responsible?"

Carla stood up. "I can tell you the guilty party is in this room." She pointed to Franck. "You, Dr. Franck, have a more intimate knowledge of my work than anyone else here."

Franck spluttered. "You cannot be serious!"

Carla shook her head. "You have been head of this department for less than a year. That rules you out. On the other hand, Major Grant, you have been here for much longer. And you are never far from this office. You and Dr. Franck seem joined at the hip. As head of security, no one would suspect you. Who would have more opportunity to steal code and who else could smuggle it out of the building?"

Grant's mouth fell open. He said nothing.

"And finally, we come to Ricarda Petrik, a Chief Finance Officer whose husband has been arraigned for a huge ponzi scheme. You have the necessary technical background, every opportunity, and more motive than most to sell XA secrets to the Southers. What do you have to say for yourself?"

"It's not true," said Petrik. "It must have been Grant."

"I would have to agree with you," said Carla, "but I believe whoever the mole was, it was someone wedded to the Souther philosophy. When we returned to Earth on the *Missie Bess*, after the pirates had taken the second freighter, my test subject, Alpha Oscar, was smuggled from the ship's cargo and taken away to a Souther lab on a flatbed hovertruck. Who among us could have organized that?" She turned to stare at Stepan, sitting at the table behind her. "Who but a docks manager could have arranged for the box containing Oscar to be off-loaded from the *Missie Bess* in LAX and spirited away? And who but a Souther agent could have made the arrangements in a Spaceport under Souther control?"

Stepan laughed. "You want to involve me in all this? What do I know about androids or code?"

"Nothing, perhaps, but we lived together for several years. You would have had ample opportunity to steal my code during that period. I often brought work home with me."

Stepan scoffed. "How could I have known which box to off-load when the *Missie Bess* docked?"

"That's easy," she said. "I saw Igor sending a message when we docked. If we check the records, I'm sure we'll find you received a signal from Igor."

"Who was it who smuggled you and your android domestic onto that freighter? Why would I have done that if I was working with the enemy?"

"I imagine it suited your purposes to have me transported to the D-System. Having me on Leninets would have been ideal from their point of view. How much did they agree to pay you to get me on board the *Archangel*?"

"You have no proof," he growled.

"Ah, but I have," said Carla. "When I told you that I had been struck on the head by an AU I told you his name was Oscar. And when I told you one of my test subjects had disappeared, you said, 'Alpha Oscar.' How could you have known his name was Alpha Oscar unless you were in contact with the Souther engineers?"

Grant strode across and placed Stepan in handcuffs.

"Damn you, Carla Scott," Stepan snarled. "I'll see you in hell."

Chapter 60

Carla found a smiling Sophie with a fully conscious Cassidy sitting up in his hospital bed. His head was still bandaged, and his right arm was still in plaster, but he was no longer attached to all the noisy monitors.

He held out a hand to Carla "Sophie told me how she rescued you from Vlad."

Carla grasped his hand. "Was that his name? He never introduced himself."

"I hear you met with the ANTIX leader, Benn. He's an impressive character, don't you think?"

"A great leader on a private crusade."

"He told me he wanted to add AUs to his team. Did he ask you to help him?"

"Yes," said Carla. "He purloined some domestic Units and, somewhat against my better judgment, I helped to enhance them."

"How many?"

She looked around the room. "I'm not sure we should be discussing this in public."

"Quite right," said Sophie. "You'll get answers to all your questions when you see Benn."

"You're planning to join the movement?" said

Chapter 61

Two days later, when Carla returned home from the lab, Lia opened the apartment door. "Welcome home, Carla. There was a call for you while you were out."

Carla checked her X-Vid. A recorded message from a smiling Elline said, "Your father is on his way. He should be with you by seven p.m. He said not to go to any trouble on his behalf."

Carla gave a whoop of delight. "Better prepare a meal for two, Lia." She remembered Lia's hydrophobia. "Let me do the water for you."

"I can do that," said Lia.

"Are you sure?"

"I am certain."

Carla kept an eye on Lia. The AU seemed to have no trouble operating the faucet. Her hydrophobia was cured!

Zack Scott arrived at the stroke of seven, carrying an enormous bunch of flowers. They avoided physical contact; the spontaneous display of pent-up affection from the freighter seemed inappropriate somehow, in her home.

Lia took the flowers and put them in water.

Carla invited her father to take a seat. He took the couch; she sat in the chair facing him. She began by asking her most pressing question. "Are you facing criminal charges?"

He shook his head. "No. Thankfully, 'Zack the Jock' never had to kill anyone, and happily, the police believed me."

"Zack the Jock? Is that what they called you?"

"Please don't spread it around." He laughed.

He told her something of his adventures as a pirate, and she told him what she'd been working on.

"And you think your Fear module might enable your androids to tap into some new emotions?"

"It's entirely possible," she said, "but difficult to predict and even more difficult to control."

"Does your friend have this new wonder module?" he said.

"Yes. Her name's Lia. I've asked her to prepare a meal for two. I hope you can stay, Father."

"Of course, Carla. Thank you."

She said, "Do we have any idea yet how the pirates could enter a Conduit without using the Gates at either end?"

He shook his head. "No one has a clue how they did that, but I believe the scientists are all over the Brazill Drive in the *Missie Bess* looking for clues."

They were communicating like distant acquaintances or old friends that had lost contact. Carla had an overwhelming compulsion to get beyond that, to reach out to her father. She got up and sat beside him. For a moment the move seemed awkward, but then he put an arm around her shoulders, and it was the most natural thing in the world.

She rested her head on his chest and let her tears flow.

Thanks for reading *The Shape of Fear*. If you enjoyed it, please write a short review. Reviews really help.

ABOUT THE AUTHOR

I write WW2 spy thrillers, detective stories and short stories. But my first love is Science Fiction. I live in Ireland.

BOOKS BY JJ TONER

Science Fiction

Eggs and Other Stories, a collection of science fiction short stories

Murder by Android, Android short story 1
Rogue Android, Android short story 2
Breadcrumbs, Android short story 3

The Shape of Fear, Android Wars – book 1

WW2 spy thrillers and other books

The Black Orchestra, a WW2 spy thriller
The Wings of the Eagle, the second spy thriller in the Black Orchestra series
A Postcard from Hamburg, the third spy thriller in the series
The Gingerbread Spy, the fourth spy thriller in the series

The Serpent's Egg, a WW2 Red Orchestra spy story

Zugzwang, a pre-war short story featuring Kommissar Saxon

Queen Sacrifice, the second Kommissar Saxon story

The White Knight, the third Kommissar Saxon story

Houdini's Handcuffs, a detective thriller featuring DI Ben Jordan

Find Emily, the second DI Jordan thriller

Printed in Great Britain
by Amazon